THE MAN WHO WOULD NOT BOW

Also by Askold Melnyczuk

Novels

What Is Told

Ambassador of the Dead

House of Widows

Smedley's Secret Guide to World Literature

Novella

Blind Angel: A Life of Rimbaud

As Editor

Selected Poems by Oksana Zabuzhko

Conscience, Consequence: Essays on Father Daniel Berrigan

On Bergstein

From Three Worlds: New Writing from Ukraine

Take Three Poetry Series

As Translator

Girls, a story by Oksana Zabuzhko

Eight Notes from the Blue Angel, poems by Marjana Savka

THE MAN WHO WOULD NOT BOW

& OTHER STORIES

ASKOLD MELNYCZUK

grand IOTA

Published by
grandIOTA

2 Shoreline, St Margaret's Rd, St Leonards TN37 6FB
&
37 Downsway, North Woodingdean, Brighton BN2 6BD

www.grandiota.co.uk

First edition 2021

Cover image: Rostyslav Luzhetskyy "Gogol, History Of Tales", used by permission
Typesetting & book design by Reality Street

A catalogue record for this book is available from the British Library

ISBN: 978-1-874400-83-7

Acknowledgments

My thanks to friends who read and encouraged these stories over the years: Tom Bahr, Peter Balakian, Sven Birkerts, John Fulton, Fanny Howe, Hanna Melnyczuk Stecewycz, George Scialabba and Tom Sleigh; and to the editors who published them: Jules Chametzky and Jim Hicks of *The Massachusetts Review;* Robert Fogarty of *The Antioch Review,* Carolyn Kuebler of *The New England Review,* Chandra Ganguly of *Speak,* and Donald Revell of *The Denver Quarterly.*

Thanks too to Katie Eelman for helping the book make its way in the world.

My fantasia on Gogol was nurtured both by the author's own works, particularly *The Overcoat,* as well as by a number of biographical and critical studies: Donald Fanger's *The Creation of Nikolai Gogol,* Edyta Bojanowska's *Nikolai Gogol: Between Ukrainian and Russian Nationalism,* Simon Karlinsky's *The Sexual Labyrinth of Nikolai Gogol,* and above all to George SN Luckyj's two monographs: *The Anguish of Mykola Hohol, aka Nikolai Gogol,* and *Between Gogol and Sevcenko: Polarity in Literary Ukraine: 1798-1847.* I was further inspired by Nikolai Gogol's *Meditations on the Divine Liturgy,* as well as by my contempt for many of Nabokov's judgments in his *Nikolai Gogol.*

And deepest thanks to my two editors at Grand Iota, Ken Edwards and Brian Marley, whose commitment to good letters shines forth in their own writing and in the care they lavish on the books they bring into the world.

For Alex

Who has power enough to proclaim that the defenders are doing the attacking, that the sentinels sleep, the trusted plunder, and those who watch over us are killers?

Cervantes

Tell time it is but motion;
Tell flesh it is but dust.

Sir Walter Raleigh

Contents

Termites

1 Crickets (Damascus)

John the Baptist's head must be the best-traveled skull in Christendom. Herod interred it on his estate until St Joana dug it up for reburial under the Mount of Olives, where it was unearthed by pilgrims in the fourth century. Later cameos in Rome, Constantinople, Petra, and Samaria brought gales of sweaty seekers to their knees. Smuggled by crusaders to France, only to be exiled by the Paris Commune, the head was saved by the mayor of Amiens, making him a national hero. Oliver Street finally caught up with it in Damascus, soon after his divorce.

What the young journalist actually saw was the shrine erected inside the sprawling Umayyad Mosque, itself the length of two football fields: marble columns, elaborately wrought ironwork and, somewhere behind it all, allegedly, the saint's head. Oliver imagined a cross between a bearded peach pit and a raisin with teeth.

Around him men lolled on oriental rugs reading books. He listened to the muffled footsteps and whispers of tourists passing a preaching imam in mid-sermon. The mosque was also where Jesus was to alight from Heaven at the end of days.

Oliver stood before the reliquary and shut his eyes. The great vitality of the dead. He folded his hands behind his back and tilted his head to the right. He was sweating. It was hot and he was feverish. He reached into the inside pocket of his white linen jacket for a Kleenex. Instead he felt something glossy he took out. He opened his eyes and looked at the photograph. Two girls, beaming at the camera. He put it away and probed his other pockets. No luck. He wiped his forehead with the back of his sleeve and closed his eyes. He hadn't slept in several nights. His hands shook, so he shoved them into his pockets again as he listened to the prayers of the faithful – offered in Arabic, French, English – braid together into a new language, evading the gravity of culture and time. After the craziness in Beirut, a calm descended, and for a moment Oliver felt he was standing at the center of the world.

Feeling a tug at his pants leg, he opened his eyes and saw a little boy with shaggy black hair. The child was cupping something in his right hand. He crooked a finger, inviting Oliver to draw closer. As Oliver smiled and bent down, his sunglasses slipped out of his jacket pocket. Before he could retrieve them, the boy opened his fist to reveal a giant black cricket which chirped once and sprang to the floor, startling Oliver, who bolted upright. The boy grinned. With his eyes on Oliver, the boy raised his small, sandaled foot and stomped, crushing the cricket. He smiled again, grabbed Oliver's sunglasses and raced off.

Oliver followed. The boy led him out of the mosque, deeper into the old quarter, down a narrow street lined with merchants selling everything from birds and old coins to sandals and spices. The buildings on either side seemed to lean in – one day the earth would shrug and they would all collapse on top of each other in a final embrace. The boy skipped along merrily, waving to shopkeepers, calling some by name. They responded with smiles and shout-outs before turning away, back to their work of cutting hair and pouring tea and showing off delicate, hand-colored illustrations plucked from nineteenth century editions of *One Thousand and One Nights*. Then suddenly the boy was gone.

Oliver paused. Where was he? Around him rose the voices of merchants and their clients haggling over rugs, squeezing oranges, fondling silver bracelets. Oliver felt dizzy. Reaching for a Kleenex, he again found only the photograph. Sweat burned his eyes. He squinted up and down the narrow street. A crowd of men had gathered in front of a store selling old electronics. He stepped toward them. The door to the store was open and he could hear surging music which appeared to come from an old color television console. He knew he should get back to his hotel, where he was to meet Ali for their afternoon trip to the refugee camp. Instead he stared over the men's shoulders at the television screen.

The screen showed a tall man in a conical brown hat and a white skirt so voluminous and long it brushed the ground. The man's eyes were closed. He seemed lost to the sound of the oud and a boy clapping a tambourine with the flat of his palm. Then the man in the white skirt crossed his arms above his chest. Slowly, he started to turn. As the pace of the music picked up, he began spinning faster. Soon he was whirling madly, his white skirt ballooning around him like an open umbrella. Faster and faster he whirled as the boy smacked the tambourine and the oud player's fingers spasmed across the strings.

2 Termites (A Few Days Earlier, in Beirut)

They were in the middle of a late supper when the first bomb went off. Everything stopped. Forks froze, eyes widened, even the candle flames appeared to stand taut.

"Welcome to Beirut," said their host, Dr El Hass, cutting short her toast without missing a beat. Wine glass in hand, she forced a smile as she surveyed the diners around the table. A linguistics professor at the American University, Dr El Hass used her robust physicality and oil-well eyes to command a group. Her fingers worried the coral around her neck as her gaze settled on Oliver.

Her name, he knew, was Dolorous. His editor in New York had told him all about her. She'd been born in Paris the year after *Lolita* was published. Her parents had gone there to study dentistry. Someone at the registry had misspelled her name, but she liked it, it was different, and she never tried to correct it. Anyway, she was a nymphet no longer – probably never had been. Her heavy brow aimed down, drawing attention to the gold and coral necklace splayed against her skin, and a blue satin blouse open one button too many. There was nothing sad about Dolorous.

She seemed to be waiting for an acknowledgment. The others – scholars, human rights workers, a U.N. bureaucrat – were either natives or old hands, lifers to the region. They were ready to click glasses and push on but the explosion had pricked the balloon of conviviality. At thirty-one, Oliver was the youngest, least credentialed member of the group. He was also hungover and jetlagged, having landed only a couple of hours earlier, with just enough time to drop off his bags before meeting his photographer, Garth, at the hotel and hurrying off to dinner. Now he felt the energy drain from the room, replaced by that nervous awareness you feel when walking through a dicey neighborhood in a strange city. Nevertheless, he gamely hoisted his glass to their host and turned back to Dr Aziz.

Conversations slowly resumed. Once more, plates were passed heaped with bamiye – okra stewed with tomatoes, onions and spices – kibbeh, mahashi, baba ganoush, and at least half a dozen dishes Oliver couldn't identify. A fleet of half-empty bowls lined the teak sidetable above which hung two abstract paintings. One in particular, pastel-colored shapes interlocking against a pale yellow background, caught Oliver's eye. "That's a Choucair," Aziz offered. He added: "The old girl's nearly a hundred years young."

They'd been talking about Baghdad, where Aziz taught literature and political science at the university. (*We're a bit under-staffed,* he'd deadpanned.) Now his eyes locked on a point in the middle distance visible to him alone. He seemed fully present and totally absent. His facial expression suggested a man long afflicted with irritable bowel syndrome. Oliver found his cratered face and W.C. Fields nose hard to look at. He had the curious sensation he was seeing himself in twenty years.

Aziz had been trying to explain about the tiny termite of debt, how a hole in the pocket expanded and grew, how easily a small sum swelled into an infestation, how if you didn't swat the principle at the first nibble of interest you were lost, for it would gnaw and it would chew until it swallowed your heart, which it would then shit out. "War is how the termites party," Aziz shrugged, patting his lips with a creased white linen napkin.

In the aftershock of the explosion, Aziz's shoulders clenched. He leaned forward. Two months earlier, Aziz whispered, his wife, who'd once sold real estate in the city's poshest neighborhoods, had been kidnapped. He hadn't heard from her since. A bodyguard drove his children to school every morning. He prayed all day he'd see them at dinner that night. The professor downed his wine.

Oliver imagined how he would have reacted had it been his wife. Ex-wife. Before she became his ex, then. It had only been about a month. His eyes swept the room as though scanning for Savanna.

"Why stay?" Oliver asked.

How could he leave with his wife missing, Aziz answered. Besides, students needed teachers. One day, even this war would end – yes, it would – and then?

"Who will teach the children? We've lost one generation already. Maybe more. We lose another, it will be impossible to get back. Not that we wish to get back ..."

Under the painting – the *Choucair*? – stood a bookcase stocked with volumes in four languages, along with a selection of American DVDs. A boxed set of *The Godfather* was prominently displayed.

Finally, Dr Aziz put down his fork and asked Oliver: "You are writing about the refugees?"

"I am," Oliver replied, passing a plate. All evening Oliver tried to keep his host from noticing he was avoiding anything uncooked. He'd been warned: stick with the mashawi, the grilled meats.

"You think the bombing's linked to Tripoli?" Oliver asked. The day before his arrival an extremist group seized control of a refugee camp north of Beirut.

Aziz nodded. "The camps are always vulnerable." Then he asked: "Your interest is in the Middle East?"

"Can't really avoid it these days," Oliver replied, setting down his fork. He proceeded to tell Aziz about Fawzi, his friend from college. Born in Lebanon, Fawzi now worked as an editor for an educational publisher in New York while his family remained in a hill town above Beirut. Fawzi's sister had been killed the previous summer by a stray missile while trying to flee the area. The two friends stayed in close touch then. When they spoke by phone, Fawzi was bitter. For years he'd been inviting Oliver to Lebanon. "It's a beautiful country," he repeated. And: "You should see what war looks like." So when Oliver's editor asked if he'd be interested in a story on refugees, Oliver was ready. He sipped the flat bubbly water.

"Our lives are different from yours," Aziz said softly, passing Oliver a dish of skewered lamb. Oliver forked a few cubes before urging it on the Egyptian woman from the UN sitting on his left. "But everything is connected," Aziz added.

Oliver studied the room, the heavy sidetable, the silver, the civility of the people. It was hard to reconcile such elegance with his image of a world shredded by suicide bombers and missiles. Where were those invisible threads linking his world to this? Then it came to him: he, they, the others. They themselves were the threads. Which made who the needle? Dr El Hass? Possibly. She was a surgeon trying to suture a wound.

Oliver couldn't – would never – tell Aziz that he'd supported both wars, that this trip was a partial expiation for what his scorn had unleashed. Not his alone, obviously.

Aziz was about to say something more but was interrupted by a loud knocking. Before Dr El Hass could make a move, the door flew open and a thin young man wearing a leather jacket and black dress pants rushed up to her. The way he let himself in, and her subsequent reaction, made it clear they were well-acquainted. His hair was wet. Droplets of rain dappled his glasses. The young man began whispering something but she put a hand over his mouth and gestured at the others. The new arrival paused and turned to the table. Dr Dolorous El Hass now raised her hand, with its heavy silver bracelet, as if to hush the room, though it was already silent. The thin young man brushed back his wet hair and began speaking in breathless Arabic.

Oliver's photographer-colleague Garth whispered a translation: "He's saying the bomb went off in a department store about half a mile from here. No one was hurt. Midnight on Sunday; safe to say this was either a warning or a provocation, not a real attack." Those took place in daylight, amid crowds.

There was something operatic about the scene: the way the young man in the black leather jacket, dotted with drops of rain, gestured as he spoke, hugging himself with his arms, then flinging them out like wings, and how the light from the chandelier bounced off his speckled glasses. Oliver felt like he was outside himself, watching a performance in which he had only a minor part. Probably jetlag.

When he finished, the fellow stood there, perspiring, staring at the diners as though awaiting applause.

Dr El Hass, who was still poised beside the young man, cleared her throat. Turning to her two American guests, she said, in a faint British accent: "I'm sorry for this introduction to our beautiful land. But I suppose it's what you expected, so maybe I shouldn't apologize. Anyway, this is how we're forced to live sometimes."

With that she smiled, leant forward and blew out the candles.

3 Americans

The cab raced down Beirut's empty streets which spread like a network of nerves through the heart of the city. A light rain pelted the windshield. "She's impressive," Oliver said to Garth, who was staring out the window.

"Dolorous? In her own way, I suppose," he answered. Oliver imagined him arching his brows before turning back to the window.

"Don't they have street lamps?" Oliver said, probing the dark for signs of life. Disoriented, Oliver worried they were circling the same neighborhood. Gradually, concern was displaced by exhilaration. He felt fully present, in his body in a way he so rarely was anymore. Which was what he wanted – to be taken out of his head. "You know where we are?" he asked Garth.

Garth turned to the window. "That's the old Holiday Inn," he pointed. "A hideout for snipers during the war."

"Aren't we on the wrong side of the green line?" Oliver asked. "Isn't that the Hezbollah camp over there?" Thousands of armed men surrounded the Grand Serail, headquarters of the Lebanese Prime Minister, protesting the government. From a distance Oliver could see tents and people moving among them. Garth shrugged: "It's a city that never sleeps."

A few blocks later, they wound through a square of boutiques of the sort you'd expect to find on the Rue de Rivoli or Fifth Avenue. Brightly lit picture windows featured mannequins stylishly coiffed, flaunting the latest fashions. Oliver watched a German shepherd squatting in the doorway of a Hermes store. "Reminds me," Garth said. "Watch out for the landmines. The Lebanese just don't scoop."

It was after two in the morning by the time they pulled up to their hotel. The Bristol lobby was empty. Oliver and Garth, who'd known each other casually from overlapping circles in New York, bellied up to the bar for a nightcap.

Two Jamesons on the rocks promptly appeared on the gleaming mahogany counter. Oliver swirled the liquid. "You going to call Cheryl?" he asked Garth. "Beirut must seem like Detroit after Kabul." Oliver had seen Garth's photographs from Afghanistan. But what did a picture really show? Shape and texture. The inner architecture of things remained invisible.

Garth emptied his glass. "Gimme Kabul over Detroit any day." Then he added: "Didn't know this was your beat. What brings you to my world?"

Oliver wasn't offended. But was it that obvious? Why was everyone inquiring about his motives? Wasn't it bad enough he'd latched onto a profession that was lurching toward extinction, threatening to leave him without prospects at the ripe age of thirty-one? Over the last few years, as paper after paper folded or downsized, Oliver had also begun adjunct teaching at the New School. The pay was shit but, to his surprise, he liked the classroom. He was good – theatrical, funny, confident even. But when this opportunity for fieldwork came his way, he leapt at it.

Oliver told Garth about Fawzi, whose family had been on the receiving end of the last "war". Oliver had called Fawzi's aunt right after landing at the airport. They'd set up a time to meet the next day.

"And Syria?" Garth asked, rattling the ice in his glass. Syria had been his editor's suggestion. It was much in the news. As long as he was in the neighborhood, he should check on the influx of Iraqi refugees pouring across the border, carrying nothing more than a suitcase.

"He's right. You should," Garth nodded. "Wake up, dude. You're about to visit the oldest fucking city on the planet. There's nothing it hasn't seen. I mean, King David conquered it. Nebuchadnezzar made it kneel. Alexander the Great. Caesar. The Kurds. The Mongols. Tamerlane. The Turks. Napoleon. These people have seen it all. And now they'll get to see you!"

"Lucky them." Oliver studied the older man's nose ring, the forearms tatted with what looked like a comic strip, a head shaved down to his pumpkin-shaped, orange-tinged skull.

"Know what else, dude? Nobody's gonna give a shit. I mean, yeah, there are the people who give humanitarian awards and the like. They'll pat you on the back. Throw you some dollars. Maybe a Pulitzer, if you do something truly crazy. But it's not like anyone who matters will listen. Bombs will still drop. 'Cause those decisions happen in another wing entirely, and the two don't speak to each other."

"Thanks for the lesson," Oliver chided, but Garth was just getting going. He raised a glass in a propitiatory gesture.

"And those other guys? The deciders? They salt their omelets with the tears of the tortured." Garth emptied his glass and pushed it across the bar. "And thank you for your service," he said to the bartender.

"So if nothing you do changes anything —" Oliver sounded like one of his own students. "Why risk your ass for a picture? For a fucking by-line?"

"Because I hate pictures," Garth shrugged, as though he'd said the most obvious thing in the world. His lips widened and contracted in a fleeting grin.

"What?"

"I became a photographer because I hate looking at pictures." He locked his eyes on Oliver. "No kidding. Far as I'm concerned, all photographs are porn. I hate the way they flatten everything. I hate the way so-called artists manipulate 'the material'. Worst of all, I hate the way people believe they know something after seeing a picture. I didn't want to be one of those guys who saw the picture and believed he knew what really happened and the only way to do that was to be the guy who took that picture, after seeing what really happened." He drained his glass and set it down, with a nod to the bartender who was relieving his boredom by stacking coasters into squat turrets crowned with shot glasses.

Oliver laughed. "Love it. Makes sense to me, brother."

Just then, another explosion rattled the glasses along the bar. It was nearly 3.00AM. The bartender cursed in Arabic. The desk clerk, sleek and silver-vested, came around the counter to stare at the television. Less than a minute after the blast, the cameras were showing broken windows and men in shadows covering their eyes. Another department store. Some disgruntled customer. Oliver was glad for the distraction.

"Where is it?" Garth asked the bartender.

"Rue Hamra. North."

"Let's go," he said to Oliver, who hesitated, pushing up his glasses.

"OK." The men set off.

Outside, the warm air buzzed with cars, sirens and voices. They followed a group of men running up the block. A crowd surrounded a store whose window had been blown out. The strobe of lights from police cars disoriented Oliver who stood to the side while Garth pushed his way up front, camera in hand. Oliver listened to raised voices speaking Arabic, French, English. A group of men at the edge of the crowd screamed at each other, but Oliver was too far away to hear what they were saying. A boy on a bicycle rode up and down the street. Shards of glass glittered along the pavement.

"Hope you got some good pictures," he said to Garth as the two headed back to the hotel. Garth wiped his forehead with the back of his hand. "Who knows?"

There were no casualties yet this second bombing of the night led the international news anyway. Oliver thought of his mother, Yulia, whose stories about *her* war suddenly felt less abstract. She'd seemed so cheerful when she told him she was marrying again. "Four's a charm," she said almost wistfully.

Back in his room, he stripped to his shorts and stretched out on the bed. He wondered what Savanna was doing. He reflected on her litany of complaints against him: that he was more absent than present; that he needed to find a full-time job (well, yeah). Was he that different from the person he'd been three years earlier, when they moved in together? He remembered the evening after the second miscarriage, how they held each other and through their sobs promised they would try again; and if that didn't work they would adopt. But plans change.

He wished he still smoked. Instead, he listened to blood breaking in waves inside him. Epinephrine surges. In time he'd acclimatise to the pressures of sea-level in Lebanon. Hormones triggered by fear floated through the air like low-lying clouds. It was what men like Garth craved: that extra oxygen in the casino. Oliver had studied the matter minutely. Biosynthesis, oxidation, methylation, dopamine.

He rose and turned the air-conditioner to high. He'd supported the Iraq war without ever having seen the enemy

– it seemed the right call at the time: to be on the winning side for once, finally a player, in the game, not always kibitzing from the sidelines. To reshape facts on the ground. Then the war turned plural, and nobody seemed to have won. He'd come here to see what he couldn't back home, make the distant dimensional. Maybe that way he'd understand more of the world that Fawzi – and his own mother, for that matter – carried inside them like a Rosetta Stone. Everything they did, whatever happened to them, they ascribed to one cause: *toujours la guerre*.

The air-conditioner rattled. He couldn't sleep, anyway. Peering behind the curtain, he saw the sky starting to whiten. He turned on his laptop and scanned *The Guardian*'s home page. Then he opened a file and made some notes. He'd been lucky to get the assignment. He had to get this story right.

*

One of the hotel's other guests, Oliver discovered at breakfast later that morning, was Aziz, the Iraqi professor he'd spoken with at dinner. He was sitting alone at the table. A dog-eared paperback lay before him, but his gaze aimed elsewhere. Dark circles shadowed his eyes, suggesting he'd slept about as well as Oliver had. Epinephrine surges were epidemic in Beirut. They should have both stayed in bed.

The dining room, on the hotel's top floor, was otherwise empty. Its glass walls opened on a deck and a pool, still and blue in the glare of middle May. The rain had stopped, the clouds cleared, and all was bathed in extravagant light. Oliver hadn't realized they were on a hill: the view unraveled all the way to the Corniche and St George Bay, before opening on the Mediterranean beyond, a blurry haze of Matisse reds and weirdly belligerent blues. He could make out figures lounging on the giant boulders rising from the sea. On the other side of the water, the French Riviera. From Oliver's present vantage point, Beirut did not look like a city under siege, and the events of the previous night seemed nothing but a bad dream.

He turned to the food. The breakfast buffet looked elaborate and slightly wilted. Oliver confined himself to yogurt, honey, and two triangles of pita. He then walked over and asked Aziz if he might join him. The older man – Oliver guessed he was in his late-sixties – rose, gave a courtly bow, and pulled back a chair. Oliver set down his plate.

"I didn't get to ask you last night, Doctor. What brings you to Beirut?"

The professor dipped a piece of cheese in a pool of honey. "Officially? I'm here to pick up some English-language books I can't buy in Baghdad. There's a new edition of *War and Peace* I want for my courses. Political science and literature: what I believe you call a 'twofer'. But also the Baker report. Not without relevance for my students."

Before leaving, Oliver himself had studied it. The Baker report was an official document authored by a former secretary of state and other senior American policy advisors from a previous administration telling the then President to get the fuck out of Iraq.

"And unofficially?" Oliver probed.

Aziz didn't answer right away. He looked down at his food then turned toward the window. Perhaps he was thinking about his missing wife. "I wanted to talk to Dr El Hass about the possibility of a teaching post here. When my wife returns," he finally said, his hands throttling a napkin.

Oliver was going to ask about the students in Baghdad, how they'd fare if their elders abandoned them. Instead, he dipped his pita into the hummus.

"Forgive me if I seem distracted," Aziz said, rubbing his forehead. "I'm waiting to hear from my daughters. They are to call as soon as they arrive at school. But, teenagers ..." The older man pulled two photos from his ragged wallet. "Salma and Leila." The girls, twelve and fourteen, were on the beach, mugging for the camera. And "Malka," Aziz said, handing Oliver a photo of the kidnapped wife.

Oliver stared at the distinguished dark-haired woman in an office chair beside a desk stacked with books, a half-smile playing over her face as though the photographer had just made a lewd remark she fully approved. "Studied business at Emory University. In Atlanta." Then Aziz asked: "Do you have children?"

Oliver, who'd been listening to the city's street – car horns, the growling of scooters, people greeting each other, as though everything were normal – shook his head, *No*.

"Ah, I'm sorry. They give meaning to everything, you know."

Oliver remembered embracing Savanna, who wept on his shoulder after the second miscarriage.

"Your wife must be worried. Mine couldn't sleep when I visited Beirut for a weekend," said the man from Baghdad.

"We're divorced."

"I'm sorry," sighed Aziz. As though Oliver were the one to be pitied. Oliver turned his head and looked out the window. He was suddenly overwhelmed by a desire to confess. Would he forgive Oliver? At that moment Aziz's phone rang, startling both men.

"Excuse me," Aziz said.

Oliver watched him wander out to the patio, speaking rapidly.

The waiter approached and asked if he wanted anything else. A Western omelet perhaps?

"*Shukrun,*" Oliver said. "No, thank you."

He then asked the waiter what he'd heard about last night's bombing. The waiter, a clean-shaven middle-aged man whose cologne seasoned the air, had positions on everything. No, it wasn't Syria or Iran, or even Israel. The American gentleman didn't understand how things were done here. This wasn't America.

"Who profits whenever a building is destroyed? Who?" the waiter asked, tilting his head.

When Oliver didn't answer him, the waiter's thin, dark-browed face lit up. He was delighted to have stumped his learned visitor who hadn't grasped what every schoolboy in Lebanon knew: It was the construction companies! "You see? You see?"

Didn't it make sense? He looked at Oliver, as though to check if the light in that dim American visage had switched on.

"Really?" Oliver finally offered.

"Of course," the man said with finality, and a curt nod of the head. "They need to make the business. Always build, bomb, build. It is very ironical."

Having achieved his mission of enlightening his guest, he turned on his heels and hurried off.

Every war was just a real estate deal gone sour. Oliver made a note.

When Aziz didn't return after a few minutes, Oliver picked up the photographs. The elder of the two girls, dark-haired and slim, had tugged back the corners of her mouth and was showing the camera her tongue, while the younger one, in a yellow bathing suit, had thrust her left foot forward, knee bent, and hoisted her left arm heavenward while her right arm paralleled the other foot, also bent at the knee as though propelling herself across sand with invisible ski poles. Oliver slipped the photographs into his pocket: he'd return them to the professor at dinner that night.

*

By 9.00AM Garth still hadn't appeared for breakfast. After scanning the deck to see whether the reluctant photographer had opted for a morning swim in the pool, Oliver went downstairs. The clerk behind the desk was the same one who'd checked them in the day before. With no more than half a dozen guests at the hotel, everyone was conspicuous.

"*As-salam Alaykom*," Oliver said. "Have you seen my friend, who was with me yesterday?"

"Ah, the photographer? *Oui, Monsieur* Garth checked out around five this morning. He left this for you, *Monsieur* Street," said the clerk.

Oliver opened the envelope: *Sorry to do this, but the real story's in Tripoli. You'll have no trouble finding some local to take a few snaps. See you back in New York. Again, sorry, but I know you'll live. And I repose in that knowledge.*

For the first time since the explosion, Oliver relaxed. He wasn't sure how his editor would react – he'd have to email immediately – but he himself felt liberated. The burden of forced collaboration lifted. He didn't share Garth's need to sniff blood.

Oliver waited in the empty lobby. Paneled in dark wood and furnished with oxblood leather club chairs, the room spoke of safety, order, continuity. It might as well have been a tony pub or a mid-level club in London. At eleven he was scheduled to meet with Ali, another of his editor's contacts, who was to chaperone them through the refugee camps.

His thoughts returned to Aziz's remarks about children. Again he felt Savanna's shoulders heaving, the sobs guttural, harsh, and throughout that first week the late-night wails of grief. They loved each other. At least they still had each other, they repeated, over and over, clutched together in the dark. And then the grief seemed to subside – until the day she told him it was over between them.

Ali arrived promptly. Red-headed and blue-eyed, he was impeccably dressed: French cuffs, polished shoes, a precisely cut pinstripe. Oliver rose to shake hands.

"Where's Mr Brown?" Ali asked.

When Oliver explained that Garth had headed north on his own, Ali's disappointment was palpable and disheartening. Thanks to his work in Afghanistan, Garth was something of a celebrity at the moment. Oliver glanced toward the hotel door, as though hoping Garth might yet sweep in.

In the end it didn't matter. As they stood there, Ali's phone rang. After a brief conversation, he frowned: "Well, anyway, it's off."

"What is?"

"Our visit to the camps in northern Lebanon."

"Why?"

"Too dangerous. When something bad happens here, it's the Americans who get blamed. Ever heard of Terry Anderson? You're the usual suspects – with good reason, sorry to say."

Anderson, also a journalist, had spent how many years in the hands of his kidnappers? Oliver couldn't recall. Anyway, the point was clear. The trip was turning into a disaster. Another email to his editor; one more reframing of the story. He reminded himself that life in the field was always unpredictable.

"What do we do now?" Oliver asked, choking down his frustration. He worried that if he didn't land this one, future assignments might become scarcer.

"We move to Syria. If things calm down, we can always return. Damascus is only two hours away."

Oliver spent the next hour composing explanatory emails to his editor and a few friends. Then he packed his bags, and called Fawzi's aunt to say he'd be in touch when he returned. He waited for Ali in the lobby, hunched over his laptop, typing furiously.

4 The Slant of Light in Damascus

The Subaru raced too quickly down a narrow, battle-scarred highway. Sweating, heavy-faced, Ali explained to Oliver he'd been a dentist until bombs destroyed the medical building where he worked. Now he cobbled together a living doing odd jobs for friends. Oliver sat beside him in the front seat of the Forester. The SUV veered around ruts and cavities as big as beer barrels. As the vehicle rocked side to side, Oliver gripped his armrest and stared out as green hills gave way to white sand.

On the road to Damascus they passed several checkpoints guarded by tanks. Driving under a bombed-out bridge, Oliver stared at the twisted girders, which reminded him of what he'd seen at the World Trade Center where he'd volunteered many a day.

Heat and sleeplessness made him glassy-eyed. In his fragile state, everything felt significant. When the white city appeared on the horizon, Oliver's heart began to race. The traffic thickened and soon they were inching through insane gridlock, past white plaster houses and white internet cafés, until they reached the ultra-chic Meridien. Here sheikhs in flowing robes, slit-skirted babes on both arms (you just run the credit card between their legs, Ali explained), streamed by under the watchful eye of the President, whose pictures were everywhere. He had been an ophthalmologist, Oliver remembered, and was only summoned to politics after his brother, the heir apparent, died in a car crash. A nation of specialists.

The hotel was next to barracks where soldiers drilled all day. The city, meanwhile, offered "spontaneous" festivals on every corner. "The government needs to keep people busy," Ali explained. "Unemployment was already high before a million and a half Iraqis began to arrive, carrying only a few suitcases and some savings. It's a delicate situation."

More refugees, Oliver thought.

In his room, which was spacious and very white, walls gleaming like reflector lamps, he showered, shaved, and changed clothes. The shower did little to refresh him. The whiteness of the room made him feel he was walking across a bare stage with all the spots on high. Through an open window he listened to soldiers barking orders as they drilled. The sense of a drum – a war drum – ceaselessly pounding. Beirut seemed sleepy by comparison. He sprawled across his bed and carefully reviewed his wallet, removing anything he'd hate to lose and burying it in his suitcase. He would need Syrian pounds from the ATM.

He had the rest of the day to himself. After getting his money, he plunged into a world packed with bodies: bound in robes and skirts and jeans. The sun glazed every surface like a pale batter. He put on his sunglasses. In blazing heat, people swayed erratically down the sidewalk and spilled into the street. No one stopped at lights, and entering rotaries was Russian roulette with five bullets in the chamber instead of just one. "Here nobody obeys traffic laws," Ali had pointed out, pitching his bald head forward toward the windshield. "They pay attention to their senses. Sometimes it's better."

Oliver headed for the Umayyad Mosque. He'd only gone a few blocks before he began feeling like he was being followed. He stopped and looked over his shoulder – he felt like a rock in the middle of a river as the steady press of pedestrians adjusted their gait to keep from knocking him over. No one he could see seemed focused on him. He went on but the feeling persisted. Again he stopped and looked around. And that was when he saw him: a giant, a head the size of a truck, and eyes like bathyspheres. On the billboard to his right. And to his left. In front of him, and over his shoulder. He was everywhere: the President, the supreme leader, the optician-cum-undertaker, the vampire-in-chief.

Entering the old city, he felt time itself slow, modified by ancient buildings whose carved stone insisted that humans recalibrate to the rhythms of geologic flesh. From a distance, the mosque, as though veiled in its own hijab, concealed its true, strange majesty and size. Facing away from it were the remaining arches of the Temple of Jupiter, on whose site it had been built. The interior courtyard, with its polished stone floor, was like a playground where men and women clustered to chat while their kids amused themselves, mostly by dipping their hands in the fountain and screaming. Families picnicked.

Walking into the mosque, Oliver was unprepared for its immensity, the way the interior space seemed to open and stretch, it seemed, for miles. The militant bluster of the outside world was replaced by an atmosphere of remarkable grace and delicacy, as though he'd stepped inside the cloud of unknowing itself. The mosque, he found, was divided into distinct zones. In one corner, an imam preached to kneeling men with flowing beards. In another, women sat in silent contemplation. Further in, hushed tourists circled the steel and glass cabinet that was alleged to house John the Baptist's head. It was like a village inside the city. He stood before the reliquary and tried to remember what he could about the prophet whose self-appointed mission had been to make ready the ground for the coming of the Lord. He didn't remember much. All he could conjure up was a shaggy man sheathed in bearskin, leaning on a staff, as he baptized Jesus in the river Jordan – and of course the story about Salome dancing for the king, and asking for John's head.

Then that boy with the cricket showed up, shaking him from his reverie. Oliver had followed him into the old city, where he lost sight of the boy – and himself. He wound up watching a white-skirted dervish whirling ecstatically on an old color TV.

In a daze, he walked through the souk, a canopied market like a medieval Walmart spreading in all directions. He kept getting lost. Every alley revealed a new swatch of colors and fresh bouquets. Baharat Boulevard was like the inside of a paint factory, vivid with dry pigment: cayenne and cumin and saffron spilling from large burlap sacks lining the alley. At one stall, he paused to finger a hand-painted illustration from the *Arabian Nights*. He held one up to the light to admire the precise inklines limning a man and a woman embracing on a divan against a backdrop of dull gold. "That you would come to us at such a time," said the scrawny, middle-aged store owner with a salaam, fingers to forehead and a low bow. "Welcome, welcome." Oliver, wiping sweat off his brow, while being careful not to stain its edges, bought the print.

Over the next week, Oliver worked with Ismail, a Syrian photographer his editor found for him. During the day they visited several "camps" – more like separate villages now, inner cities within inner cities, the tents long replaced by concrete boxes. One, inside Damascus itself, reminded Oliver of Paterson, New Jersey: overcrowded, chaotic, discouraging, yet *there*; others were still more rudimentary. Hordes of kids scampered through the alleys. These children knew death front to back; you saw it in their eyes. Love, too. It escaped around the edges of their irises. Their mothers loved them. Whoever hurt their mothers hurt them. So it went, the cycles of hurt. No one forgot; no one forgave. He listened to elders complain about sewage and water. Familiar grievances in the so-called developing world. (Did anyone wonder any more what it was developing into?) What struck Oliver was the continuity of the narrative: one gray-bearded gentleman in flowing robes showed him the key to his house in Bethlehem; another sent a nephew to dig up a deed. Unfolding it, the man pointed to a brown stain he said was his mother's blood.

At the end of each day, Ali, the driver, excused himself to go home. Ismail, thirty and educated in Paris, took Oliver to clubs where they drank arak and smoked hubbly bubbly. They didn't talk much, which suited Oliver, who enjoyed watching the women dance.

Later, in bed, Oliver listened to blood's martial rhythm in his ears while images from the day washed over him. In one small concrete house fifteen people lived. Children kept passing through the room where he and Ali and Ismail sat on the carpeted floor, backs against the wall, speaking with men from the community. Ismail took pictures while Oliver made notes. He knew the world did not want to see this. Everyone had troubles of his own. What good did it do, knowing the sorrows of strangers five thousand miles away?

And then he thought of his own mother, and his grandparents whom he'd known only from Yulia's stories. He remembered her talking about the friends of hers who'd been arrested. One had been shot right in front of her. She'd seen entire neighborhoods razed by bombs. The word *trauma* had never come up in their conversations, yet surely she bore scars.

He was sitting up now. It was one in the morning. He was naked and the air conditioner was on but he was sweating anyway. His fever was breaking. Suddenly he felt chilled. He rubbed his forearms like he hoped they might catch fire. He got out of bed and stretched his arms over his head. Maybe he should try whirling. If you couldn't get it right here, Oliver thought, with all the wisdom of the ancient world behind you, what could you expect from the rest of the world? Through the thick window pane he could hear the military continuing their drills.

Giving up on sleep, Oliver dressed and went down to the bar. He ordered a Jameson and looked around. The dark room buzzed with voices speaking French, German, Japanese, Arabic. Robes and suits blended happily, offset by girls in dresses like nighties. He walked out into the hall.

Middle Eastern music accompanied by clapping filtered from a room behind the elevator. Following the sound, Oliver entered an intimate club with small tables set out in a semicircle below a blazing chandelier. In the open area, a woman in a thin, gold-sequined halter was belly dancing. The audience was almost entirely male. Her belly muscles rippled like waves. A tissue of sweat made her dark skin shine like velvet in the harsh, bright light.

"Watch how they treat their women," his ex once advised him. "That's the key to understanding a culture."

As he stood in the doorway, he felt something pressing against the back of his thigh. He turned around. A slim young woman with lashes like black ferns smiled at him. She leaned her hips into his thigh. "Hello," she whispered, her voice unexpectedly low for such a slip of a girl. Before he could say anything, a hand circled his wrist. Her fingers feathered his palm which she then quickly pressed between her legs before releasing it, all the while staring up at him from under lush, dark bangs.

*

Next morning he rose before five. The girl was already gone. For the first time in months he felt clean. Purged. He and the girl understood each other perfectly. Their tenderness was spontaneous, mutual, and impersonal. But it was what he had been looking for, the recognitions intuitive and skilled.

He turned to the window: bright as noon. He squinted and rubbed his eyes. Time for new glasses.

Oliver showered, dressed, and was about to go out when he noticed a manila envelope someone had slipped under the door. He opened the door and looked down the hall: empty but for a waiter carrying a silver tray to a room at the other end of the corridor. Then he sat back down on the bed and opened the envelope.

14 September 1983

BRINGING REAL MUSCLE TO BEAR AGAINST SYRIA

Summary:

Syria at present has a hammerlock on US interests both in Lebanon and in the Gulf -- through closure of Iraq's pipeline thereby threatening Iraqi internationalization of the war. The US should consider sharply escalating the pressures against Assad through covertly orchestrating simultaneous military threats against Syria from three border states hostile to Syria: Iraq, Israel and Turkey. Iraq, perceived to be increasingly desperate in the Gulf War, would undertake limited military (air) operations against Syria with the sole goal of opening the pipeline. Although opening war on a second front against Syria poses considerable risk to Iraq, Syria would also face a two-front war since it is already heavily engaged in the Bekaa, on the Golan and in maintaining control over a hostile and restive population inside Syria.

Israel would simultaneously raise tensions along Syria's Lebanon front without actually going to war. Turkey, angered by Syrian support to Armenian terrorism, to Iraqi Kurds on Turkey's Kurdish border areas and to Turkish terrorists operating out of northern Syria, has often considered launching unilateral military operations against terrorist camps in northern Syria. Virtually all Arab states would have sympathy for Iraq.

Faced with three belligerent fronts, Assad would probably be forced to abandon his policy of closure of the pipeline. Such a concession would relieve the economic pressure on Iraq, and perhaps force Iran to reconsider bringing the war to an end. It would be a sharp blow to Syria's prestige and could effect the equation of forces in Lebanon.

Syria continues to maintain a hammerlock on two key US interests in the Middle East:

-- Syrian refusal to withdraw its troops from Lebanon ensures Israeli occupation in the south;

-- Syrian closure of the Iraqi pipeline has been a key factor in bringing Iraq to its financial knees, impelling it towards dangerous internationalization of the war in the Gulf.

Diplomatic initiatives to date have had little effect on Assad who has so far correctly calculated the play of forces in the area and concluded that they are only weakly arrayed against him. If the US is to rein in Syria's spoiling role, it can only do so through exertion of real muscle which will pose a vital threat to Assad's position and power.

After finishing the last page, he got up and looked out the window. Across the street, the soldiers had already started to drill. Someone was trying to give him a history lesson. He looked down at the date. The paper was decades old yet much of it could have been written yesterday. He needed some air.

A few blocks from the hotel, he wandered into a residential neighborhood. The low buildings, of light-colored sandstone, were new, and the wide, freshly paved street looked like it had just been vacuumed. He didn't think of himself as naïve, but this was "the Middle East", a place where history extended to the very beginnings of history itself. You could read all the books you wanted about the past and still know nothing. You could talk to all the people you wanted to but you could never talk to everyone, and the one person you missed might well hold the key. When it came to the present, well, he wasn't sure how others reached their conclusions but he himself had preferred to trust people he believed had information he didn't. He wouldn't make that mistake again anytime soon.

A car horn interrupted his reverie. He looked up and down the pristine street. Not a soul in sight. Only a cat wailing its woes to the world. There it was, hurrying along the gutter with something in its mouth. Patched orange, black, and white, it looked like a regional map. Without knowing why, Oliver followed it. After a block, it paused below the front fender of a blue Mercedes, dropped whatever it was carrying, and caterwauled. As Oliver crouched to examine the delivery, the cat locked its eyes on him and keened. He leant closer. The little body curled under the tire belonged to a newborn kitten. Then he noticed two other kitten bodies under the car.

Oliver rose and headed back to the hotel. After breakfast,

he sat down in the lobby and waited for Ali and Ismail. He thought about the cat and the dead kittens. What happened? What lies behind any seemingly simple scene inside the fleet tableau of daily life: the sad clerk at the CVS counter handing him a scroll of useless coupons, the reasonably well-dressed man with a yellow backpack from Eastern Mountain Sports hawking *Spare Change* in front of a boutique clothing store, the pretty woman with the bandana on the subway clutching two young children in either hand – how did they prepare for the moment he crossed paths with them? Had the cat killed its own kittens? Oliver thought about his mother. Did others enjoy their terrible lives as much as they pretended to? He drummed his fingers on the round mahogany table and sipped his coffee.

*

"Mr Oliver?"

Sunk in a plush leather chair, he had been thinking: If domestic life had worked out for him, if Savanna's heart had stayed open, if they'd had children, would he have ever found himself in Damascus? Was that how it was for every soldier of fortune?

Now Oliver found himself staring into the dark, wide face of a man with a heavy moustache and soul patch, the terracotta skin scarred by adolescence. "Yes?"

"I am your driver today," the man announced.

"Where's Ali?" Oliver asked, raking his fingers over his face.

"Sick. Back tomorrow. He hopes."

"Ismail?"

"Sick too." Again his monotone didn't invite investigation. "I am Hicham," he shrugged: take it or leave it. Black suit, white shirt, open-collared, crisp. Uniforms imposing order on internal chaos. Why did this feel like a set-up? What lesson was he about to receive? Despite his suspicions, Oliver said nothing; then gathered himself.

"Where are we going today?" This was to be the last trip before his departure.

"Golan Heights."

Yes, the Heights. The plateau and mountain range Israel occupied since the '67 war. He'd heard the words so often he almost felt he'd been there. But as the rugged gold landscape unfolded under the wheels of the Subaru, he understood he was being taken to see the place for a reason. He sat upfront, next to Hicham, who chain-smoked Gitanes. Oliver wondered what it felt like to Hicham: assigned to chauffeur an utterly unimportant visitor from the heart of an empire that had labeled the man's country part of "the axis of evil". To know that your passenger belonged to the tribe that threatened your very existence. He sensed Hicham trying to make himself smaller, less obtrusive, less of a target. Before heading out, Hicham said he needed to call his daughter to make sure she was ready for school. When Hicham hung up, he reached into his wallet and showed Oliver a photograph of Salma.

"We will go to Quintera," Hicham explained as they headed out. The day before they'd visited Bosra, with its intact Roman amphitheatre and the ruins of a church said to be the inspiration for St Sophia in Istanbul. Fragments of history assembled into a surreal collage.

Throughout the hour-long journey, the driver spoke about the way Israel had destroyed the Middle East. Oliver found it hard to listen to. He eyed the pale gold landscape. The longer the driver went on, the more resentful Oliver became. He resented being put in a position where he was expected to judge, almost as much as he hated having others judge for him. Then, as they neared Quintera and he saw the cars of the Syrian military, he began wondering if someone had told the authorities.

Again he was seized by an insane desire to confess everything, tell his hosts how he screamed at the set when the bombs began to fall, Yes, yes, yes. He had wanted it to end quickly, everything problematic vaporized, gone, never to be thought of again. Many of his friends, most of whom were otherwise run-of-the-mill liberals, had taken a similar stance.

Shuddering, he looked at the driver: surely they knew who he was; they knew what he thought. Hicham's eyes were locked on the road, a narrow strip of black flanked by golden fields of sand, and then he was slowing down, pulling over.

Don't be paranoid, Oliver told himself. Surrounded by endless stretches of nothing, his heart pounded: really, it wouldn't have been hard to check his blog from last summer. It was reading Oliver's blog that upset Fawzi, his college friend. *How could Oliver be so glib*, he wrote. Fawzi had reached out to Oliver. "Flesh out an abstraction," he said. "We're not cartoons. When you cut us, we bleed. When you bomb us, we die."

Quintera was a museum: an unreconstructed village battered by the Israelis forty years earlier. The gray concrete shells of the buildings were studded with bullet holes. They looked like a decayed gray cheese. Oliver was the only visitor that morning. He wandered between buildings, the driver his shadow a few feet behind, offering commentary: This used to be a hospital; this was once a church. There, across the border, stood Israel. Look how green. The soil so fertile. Because of the lake and the mountains. The Golan Heights were all about water.

He had heard it over and over: religion was an excuse. The wars in the region were about water, land, oil. What was it the waiter had said? Every war was just a real estate deal gone bad? How ordinary it appeared, this swatch of territory commanding the attention of millions.

Standing in the shell of a bombed-out church, Oliver heard footsteps behind him, grinding the stone and hard clay. They'd finally come. He knew it. He was to be executed. He'd known it all along. But when he whirled around he saw no one, not even his driver, who appeared to have walked away for a smoke.

Leaving the church, he wandered down the hill, over the crusty pale ground – like walking on walnuts – when he saw something glinting in the sand. He hunched down and picked it up between his fingers. A bullet casing! He held it up to the light. What kind of gun did it come from? Oliver had no idea. He put it in his pocket and turned to look for Hicham.

And that was when he saw them: half a dozen soldiers, rifles raised and pointing at him. This time he wasn't imagining it. He immediately threw up his hands.

"What are you doing here?" shouted a thin young soldier, sporting that ubiquitous Hussein moustache.

"I'm a journalist, a journalist," Oliver stuttered, knowing his profession wasn't any guarantor of protection in this part of the world. Or anywhere, anymore, actually.

The young man broke out of the circle and stepped toward him. He lowered his rifle; his dark brows opened and closed like a drawbridge. The thumping of Oliver's heart was temporarily drowned out by the sensation of warmth from the urine streaming down his thigh.

"Knees," barked the soldier. "Knees!"

Oliver sank down. The man approached, crouched down, gun lowered.

"You are American?" he shouted. Oliver felt his breath on his face.

"I'm here with Ali. You know Ali?" Oliver said, his voice pitched high and cracking. Then he remembered it wasn't Ali but Hicham who drove him here. "Hicham. I meant Hicham."

The soldier stood up, took a step back and chuckled: "Ali? I know many Alis. Many Hichams, too. You have identification?"

"Sure, sure," Oliver said, dropping his right hand into his back pocket, only to find it empty. Shit. His wallet was in his bag in the van. His eyes locked on the gun at the soldier's side. So this was how it would end. Hadn't he dreamt this? He was sure he had; it felt like déjà vu.

The sun burned his cheeks and forehead. He patted himself down, searching for his wallet. Reaching into his inside jacket pocket, he pulled out a photograph. Where had it come from? Aziz's daughters. Without thinking, he brought the photo to his lips and kissed it.

"Give it, give it!" the soldier commanded. It was then Oliver noticed the arm holding the rifle was trembling. The kid was probably as scared as he was. Which made him even more dangerous.

The soldier gestured to one of the other men, who lowered his rifle, came forward, and took the photograph. He held it up to his face. Oliver felt a pressure in his bowels. One way or another, this was going to be a messsy affair.

Oliver shut his eyes. He never expected a firing squad. Something else. His heart beat rapidly as images flowered under his lids: he saw himself sinking into the earth, which had become bubbling cauldron of brown mud writhing with insects, caterpillars, beetles, centipedes, even moths, all vivid orange and red and green, flapping wings and roiling crimped legs in the soil. The image appeared nightmarish, yet to his surprise he was flooded with a feeling of supreme calm. A sensation of wellbeing suffused his entire body. All was well, and would continue to be well, because everywhere he looked, every millimeter of space, the visible and the invisible, the matter he saw and the dark matter he didn't, hummed with life, heedless and self-delighting, and his death would be nothing more than a re-entry into the feverish stew.

When, after a few seconds, nothing happened, he opened his eyes to see the soldier grinning as he handed the photograph to the group's apparent leader, himself surely no older than twenty. The kid held it up to his face and soon he too was smiling. He said something to the other soldier, who took back the photo and passed it among the others. Studying it, each man grinned and nodded approvingly.

At that moment Oliver's driver, Hicham, appeared at the top of the hill. Seeing his charge on his knees with his hands in the air, he shouted something. The young soldier whirled around. Hicham kept shouting. The soldier stood his ground. Hicham approached, all the while releasing a stream of what Oliver assumed were curses. The other soldiers watched tensely as the two faced off. Finally the commander, who had turned red, barked an order. The men lowered their rifles and backed off.

On the return trip to Damascus, Oliver listened to Hicham's litany of grievances. His heart grew heavier with every mile, every explicitly enumerated abuse. Britain did this and France did that. Then it was Israel and the United States.

Oliver nodded. He agreed: the sins of empire were long, and its heartlessness inscribed a history no one could read without tears. Yes, Oliver felt that now. There was no denying it. But where and how would it end? Then Hicham made his proposal, and Oliver felt like something long and metallic had been shoved up his back.

5 History is Too Much Trouble

His last evening in Syria, at a restaurant above the city, Oliver listened to Ismail's story about Mohammed gazing down from that same hill and refusing to descend into the valley. He couldn't bring himself to enter Damascus. Mere mortals weren't meant to walk in Paradise. Then Ismail added, "Abel's tomb is just a few miles east of here." East of Eden. He thought about the CIA report he'd read. Eden had seen better days. Done working, Oliver dropped his guard. He drank a lot of wine. At last he let himself sink into the mythical swoon infecting the region. He'd been resisting it. But he was in Cain's neighborhood. Jesus. For eight thousand years, people had lived and died here. Gods and prophets strode these hills. Enveloped in an expanding universe of associations, Oliver forgot all about Garth, his ex-wife, his job. He surrendered to the spell holding so much of the world in its thrall. Light and heat burned time away. He awoke outside it, in a space where the human bordered something eerie. Ridiculous, he thought: heat stroke and red wine; rhetorical hallucinations obscuring the place as it was – a region whose underground resources belied the blinding emptiness above.

He told Ismail that Hicham had asked him if he wanted to join the resistance. Resistance? Oliver had asked. To the source of all our problems. Which was? Capitalism. The guy wanted him to sign on to some kind of Marxist plot. Ismail arched a skeptical brow. Well, he said, I don't know about any plot, but you'll admit we have a problem that's systemic, no?

Oliver sighed. There was a flaw in a system which throve on so much death and destruction. Without socialism, there will never be peace, Ismail added, which Oliver thought strange, given he lived in a dictatorship. But maybe that was the point.

He said nothing to Ismail about what had shaken him most about the whole experience: his life had been spared thanks to someone else's children. The men didn't pursue the economic debate any further.

His hosts decided it wasn't safe to return to Lebanon. He was re-routed through Damascus Airport instead. Before leaving, he wrote Fawzi's aunt a note of apology.

6 Piercing and Beautiful

Oliver returned to a shitstorm. It began, not as he'd expected, with his mother, but with this father.

Oliver been home less than a week when his father, who lived alone in Garwood, New Jersey, had a heart attack on his way to the Stop and Shop up the street. Slammed into the Tasty Freeze on North Avenue. No one else was hurt, but by the time the ambulance delivered him to the emergency room at Overlook he was dead.

In the flurry that followed the funeral – a whirl of paperwork, his distraught mother – he lost the thread of his project. He missed three deadlines for filing the refugee story before his editor told him to bag it. Oliver protested, promising he'd finish by the end of the week. He stayed up all night but the piece refused to come together. He kept returning to the cat. He tried to focus on the people but the cat shadowed his narrative. He wasn't thrilled by what he emailed Friday morning and he wasn't surprised when, this time, his editor rejected it flat-out, no further discussion. A disheartened Oliver threw himself into getting ready for the fall semester. He had a new course to prepare.

He would find a way to show his students the medium still mattered – there were things, important things, only words could get across.

The halogen torchiere lit his study late into the evening as he annotated his McLuhan, drawing on a steady supply of Sam Adams for support. This was where he felt happiest, he thought – not in the field but in his study. Alone, he talked to himself. Now and then he interrupted his work to kick back with a pricey cigar. A photograph of Orwell watched serenely from the bulletin board above his rolltop desk.

One night in late July, he woke at three in the morning from a nightmare. He'd dreamed he'd been running through the Umayyad Mosque and had knocked over the reliquary. Out tumbled John the Baptist's head. It rolled across the carpeted floor. When he reached it, he noticed it had a full scalp of thick brown hair and a long, stringy beard. Bending closer, he saw its eyes were open, the lips moving. The head was trying to speak. He pressed his ear to its mouth. Instead of prophecy and revelation, he felt something wet and clammy licking his outer lobe. When he turned to face the head, it spat in his eye.

Oliver sat up in bed and listened to what sounded like someone knocking over a garbage can outside. Unable to get back to sleep, he went to the kitchen and pulled one of his father's bottles of Seagram's off the shelf. He'd brought it back as a memento. He'd loved his father and he missed him now more than ever. He hadn't had such shitty whiskey in years. He wondered if his writing career would ever get back on track. He refilled the tumbler and stood there, looking out the half-window through which he often studied the many ways humans armored their feet. An aluminum trashcan rolled into view and suddenly he found himself gazing at a raccoon the size of a small child. The raccoon sensed it was being watched. It lifted its intelligent head in his direction. There was something about the body, coupled with the black circles around its eyes, that made him think of Aziz, the Iraqi professor. He wondered if his wife had ever been found.

Enough, he said to himself. Things had to change. By the end of the summer, however, nothing had.

*

A year passed. The following September, Garth's volume of photographs from the Middle East appeared. The book had just been blessed by the *Sunday Times Book Review*, which Oliver read over a late-Monday-night dinner at the old Cornelia Street Café.

How had Garth managed to get the book out so quickly, he wondered?

The photographs were "piercing and beautiful". Oliver grunted at the phrase. Aestheticizing tragedy. His own rejected piece, along with hundreds of pages of notes, lay in a box under his desk. Envy was an unwelcome emotion. He did not envy envy.

The semester was going well. And he'd recently begun seeing a new young hire in sociology. She was playful. Play was what he needed more than anything. He decided to stop in the lingerie store around the corner and surprise her. She seemed ready for a surprise. He wiped his mouth with a cloth napkin and pushed back his empty plate. The slim, dark-haired waitress, likely a student, perhaps even a cellist – he didn't know why that occurred to him – appeared with the check. Her smile incited a pang.

He pulled some quarters from the change the cellist left and tilted down into the oily autumn air.

He walked to the next block and slipped into the lingerie store. Inside the Pink Pussycat he was confronted by an array of singular objects: there were cock rings, condoms, and clit clamps. He beheld butt plugs and dildos modeled on the penises of famous porn stars. He walked down aisles of strap-ons, inflatables, and anal probes. He studied a tiny vibrator-like instrument called a rabbit. Two young women in plaid skirts entered the shop. His heart beat faster – not in shame, in excitement.

He settled on a pair of heavy silver handcuffs. Before stepping out, he buried his treasure deep in his bag.

He wasn't far from Seventh Avenue, near Sheridan Square, where he'd found a rare parking space.

Reaching into his pocket for his keys, he heard someone shout his name:

"Oliver!"

It was his friend Fawzi, whom he'd avoided ever since returning from Damascus.

Fawzi bounded up to him, all smiles, shiny like he'd just come from a fluff and buff. He'd married recently. First time. The invitation had arrived months ago. Oliver threw it out, just as he ignored the half dozen phone messages Fawzi had left on his machine soon after he arrived home.

He stared at his friend. Fawzi's face dazzled with the soft light of a deep happiness. Oliver could barely stand to look at him.

He felt smaller by the minute. Before taking Fawzi's hand, he slipped the book review from his jacket pocket into his bag. In the process, the pink package from the Pussycat fell to the sidewalk. The handcuffs slipped out. He grabbed them and buried them back in his bag.

Across the street a fat man wearing a Santa suit wobbled along the sidewalk.

"Fawzi, how are you?" He forced a smile.

"Oliver, my friend, why have you been hiding from me?"

Best take the business head on.

"I felt bad, Fawzi. It didn't work out. I never got to visit your aunt."

"I know, I know, she called me. I'd already heard about Nahr al Bared. I was worried about you. That's the way it is there. I'm sorry you had such bad luck. But that's no problem. You know I called you a dozen times, right? I was afraid something was wrong with you and Savanna."

"No worse than it ever was."

"She'll soften. You'll see."

Fawzi was one of the only people to whom he'd spoken about what had happened. Fawzi never appeared to doubt him.

"Did you ever write anything?"

"I tried, Fawzi. But you know my father died, and then the semester ..."

"I'm sorry, my friend." Fawzi put a hand on Oliver's shoulder and squeezed it.

"Life only. But hey, congratulations, man."

"Thanks, thanks a lot."

No resentment. No questions about why he hadn't come.

"You look happy, Fawzi."

"I am."

"That's good. Everyone deserves to be happy."

"At least some of the time," Fawzi added.

They stood in silence awhile. The weight of all that was unsaid, that could no longer be said, rose around them.

Fawzi finally broke the spell.

"Great seeing you. Listen, don't be a stranger. Deirdre's dying to meet you."

Oliver tried to smile.

"It's good to see you, Fawzi. I'll call. I promise."

Oliver crumpled into his Civic. He tossed the bag onto the back seat. Then he put a newspaper over it so he wouldn't have to see it in the rear-view. He wondered about Dr Aziz and his daughters. He hadn't thought of him for a long time. All his good intentions – about being an agent of change and making a difference – had receded under the ever-urgent press of daily life.

When he started the car, the radio blared Big Band music while a little beeping noise brought his attention to the dashboard. A red light indicated the driver's side door was open. He threw it wide and was about to yank it shut when a Budget rent-a-truck slammed into it, almost taking his arm with it. The truck grumbled indifferently up Seventh Avenue. Meanwhile, the "Chattanooga Choo Choo" roared on.

His car door lay on the street half a block away.

Oliver wasn't going to let this pass. He leaped out heedlessly, ignoring the traffic.

"Motherfucker!" he cried.

Returning to the car, he switched off the engine, removed the key and put it in his pocket. He hurried over to the door and dragged it up onto the sidewalk. Ignoring the staring strangers, he dropped it and kept walking. He walked up Seventh Avenue, past a basketball court, the Galway Hooker, the Tanti Baci Café, and a store that sold African masks. He stopped at a light. Nearly everyone around him was chattering into a cell phone. Something was wrong. Something was missing. He could feel it. There was a hole in the heart of the city. The light changed. The traffic surged. He let the crowd carry him forward. The noise of his city surrounded him until, for the time being, he could hear nothing else.

Walk With Us

You put yourself in a position – you make yourself available – and you really are no longer responsible for your actions, you've given yourself over to a force greater than you, and it's not God, and it's not good. We had the bad luck to see this happen to our child. And now it's too late.

I tried explaining this to Gibbs, but he's not buying it. First he made me speak louder until I was almost yelling. Last night a bug crawled into my husband's ear. I have to raise my voice, to which he turns a confused and slightly panicked face, like he's wondering if the bug's nesting there. We saw a show about houseflies sidling up to crickets and pretending to clean themselves, but what they're really doing is discharging larvae which quickly crawl into the creature then slowly eat it alive from within. His eyes dilate: it's the look I remember after our first kiss thirty years ago.

When my words finally register, he shakes his head.

He's hung up on individual responsibility, Emersonian self-reliance and all that Yankee crap I also grew up with and which is of no use today. While he's making pasta I tell him: It's your responsibility to deal with your regret; it's not your job to judge our daughter. In profile his face has that gaunt, hawk-nosed look of those great 19th century moralists. Then he executes the garlic like he was Robespierre, or Jeffrey Dahmer.

My name is Marie. Gibbs and I have lived in the same house, in a small town north of Boston, for over thirty years.

One of the many charms of the place is its history. Paul Revere galloped through on his way to Concord. Governor Winthrop briefly farmed a few blocks away. But the thing we're proudest of: "Jingle Bells" was written here. Almost for sure. There's some dispute with a village of congenital liars in Georgia I won't bother you with.

Gibbs stirs his tomato sauce, adding eight large basil leaves he removes before ladling it over the pasta.

"Looks dee-lish," I cry, all but cupping my hands to be sure he hears.

He wipes his fingers on the stiff red apron I bought him some Christmases ago.

"Think we'll see Zack tonight?"

Zack's our second born. He's studying at the junior college while working part time. He moved out a year ago but lately he's taken to dropping by every few days to rant. I worry.

"I hope not," I say.

This morning, on my way to the drugstore, I was confronted by a hundred people in wheelchairs racing down the street. I froze. All ages, colors, shapes, and sizes, they rolled on. A number of them were on the sidewalk. I had to duck into the doorway of the bank to let them pass. An old man with a wagon full of grocery bags behind him glared at me as if I had no business walking here. It took me a minute to remember that Eunice Shriver, who started the Special Olympics, died recently. A memorial march! And you know what I thought? How lucky they were. Their only problem is they can't walk, whereas I, on the other hand, can no longer breathe. Immediately I felt horrible. Why wasn't I proud of them?

We were always proud of our daughter, Sheila 2. She's named for my mother, who's seventy-three and lives outside Edinburgh. I've just finished packing for our trip there, even though we don't leave for another ten days. We fly out right after we visit our daughter in California.

I say we're proud of her, then I think: for what? Being our daughter?

Must have been an ordeal, for sure.

What will I say to her now, under the circumstances?

Before sitting down, Gibbs turns on the radio so we won't have to force the conversation. It's a repeat of the morning's roundup of the week's big news. This time all the chatter is about healthcare, only it's so loud it's likely to start a debate with the neighbors.

Suddenly Gibbs begins yelling over the radio. "Got the DVD of Benny Goodman?"

"For tonight?"

"We're packed."

"I have work."

"I don't," he replies, then sticks his little finger in his ear. "But what I wanted to say," he continues shouting, "was that as I was checking it out I said to the clerk, who's all of eighteen, 'It's important to stay in touch with the old music.' Because I was embarrassed – not by the disc but by how old I was. It was a stupid remark and I knew it but the kid came right back with: 'Yes, sir. It is.'"

On top of everything else, Gibbs is bruised because of his trumpet. Before any of this began, he'd been in a midlife tailspin which led him to reach for the brass. It was the instrument he'd always wanted to play. For his birthday he went to Osman's in Arlington and returned with a Bach B-Flat for three grand. At least it's not a sports car, he pointed out. Embouchure became the new vocabulary word around our house. Red slide grease found its way to our sheets. But he couldn't develop his mouth muscles. No matter how hard he tries, his lip trembles. At his last lesson he expressed frustration with his own limits. Naturally, being a teacher himself, he expected his instructor to murmur something conciliatory and inspiring, along the lines of *Good boy, Gibbs, always trying to better yourself.* Instead, Paul looked at him and said, "Gibbs, you're right. You're a nice guy, but your mouth ... it's not gonna happen."

This will be my first time in a prison. Gibbs used to volunteer at Walpole through the university where he teaches as an adjunct. He's tried to prepare me, but I suspect this will be different.

As a girl, I hated uniforms. In Catholic school (we weren't Catholic but the school was better than the public one) I envied the kids in the neighborhood who wore jeans and minis and halter tops. Not that I wanted to go that far – though who knows? Even today my instinct on seeing someone disguised in official garb is to yank out their shirt tail. In the high school where I teach sociology to juniors, I'm partial to the slobs.

There's a knock at the door as Gibbs scrapes the dishes. Almost immediately it opens and Zack marches in, waves of rage radiating from the red hair whose coiled filaments bristle and float like he's buffed it with a balloon.

Gibbs and I both walk quickly toward the living room, as though there's a chance we might keep him from invading our evening. "Seen this?" he hisses, tossing the newspaper on the couch. We have. It's an editorial about our daughter in a national newspaper, calling her crime "monstrous".

The crime is now more than a year old but they just moved her to California to get ready for the trial. It's the first time we'll be allowed to see her. The upcoming proceedings have, predictably, rekindled interest among journalists and pundits.

What she did is indeed monstrous; I don't live in denial. Neither do I wallow, as is Zack's way. What began as a tendency to sympathize with the suffering has blossomed into a professional surrogate martyrdom which keeps him from shaping his own life. He even compared himself to one of those medieval sin-eaters: supposedly holy people who took the transgressions of their neighbors onto themselves. Self-serving BS; he's livid neither of us will buy into it.

"It's time you made a statement," he says in his nasal whine.

I look at Gibbs, who doesn't have to raise an eyebrow for me to know how he plans to handle this.

Zack was a beautiful boy. His orange curls dangled over his shoulders until kindergarten – my father was a redhead. We treated him like a prince. Yet the minute we sent him out into the world, we started losing him. There's clearly something we did not provide that he needed. His adolescence was passed in obsessive pursuit of causes, from Cobain to Kabbala to PETA.

It's not enough that Gibbs agrees with him – though he does it Gibbs style, quietly, with an easy dignity. Zack wants to hear me say it too. Is it sibling rivalry still?

"After we see her," Gibbs says. "That will be the time for a statement."

"You have any idea what people are saying?" His voice is shrill.

"We know."

"I had a man I hardly know say to me at work," (our son's the part-time counter guy at Boloco – the only non-Spanish-speaking employee they have, I think) "'Your sister's a hero.'"

He gazes at us in disbelief. His wide-eyed stare reminds me of a photograph I once saw of Lenin after his stroke, when he could no longer speak and had to watch what he'd begun change to a nightmare right in front of him.

"We've waited a year. Another week won't matter to anyone. Except maybe to her. And to us."

Zack's right, though – one of the shocks around this tragedy is how many people support what Sheila did, saying she should have gone further. I share my son's dismay at this.

"Don't!" I snap when he moves to light a cigarette.

"Are you for real?" he scowls.

It's a good question, one I've asked myself a lot lately.

"I'll let you know when we get back from California," I say, taking off the gloves.

It's just a matter of minutes before some inane remark sends him scurrying back to JP, where he'll regale his roommates with tales of our awfulness. And for this to be happening to us, I'm starting to think, he must be right. Honestly, I'd like to light a cigarette myself.

Our daughter Sheila helped torture three people, two of whom died as a result. One of the victims was a woman. *A woman.* Dogs, electrodes, and whatever they use when they waterboard. I have a nightmare image of her riding a surfboard on a girl's head.

After dinner, relieved by Zack's departure, I sit down to check my email while Gibbs finishes the dishes. As a volunteer at the local nursing home this summer, I want to make sure Robin, my sub, understands the schedule.

Yesterday, entering the Stop and Shop, my back seized up. I froze just inside the door, blocking the entrance for a moment. The woman behind me barked like she was channeling Rin Tin Tin and suddenly I felt old. She brushed past without an apology, muttering. The way we treat the elderly – as though we can't grasp they are us, in a minute or two.

I turn on the computer. "Virgos love tequila" – the catchy non-sequitur welcomes me as I log on. Do they? Virgos, I mean. If so, what's the corollary? Are all Virgos alkies? I imagine millions of Virgos who've never had a drink in their lives mixing up batches of margaritas and saying, Yes, this is what's been missing.

You forget why you logged on in the first place.

Gibbs plods in to say I should get to bed, we're leaving early. Why? The plane's not until 6.00PM. We have the whole day.

He's called the cab already. That's Gibbs for you. My greatest error; my unspoken sin.

I tell him I'll be at least another hour; I'll sleep on the plane. I no longer look forward to sleep the way I once did. Sometimes I wake up in the middle of the night with the thought: I've got to explain the origins of evil in the world, and I'm thinking of my own daughter. What will I say to her, really? How can I make her believe I understand, even if I don't?

Gibbs is in bed with Benny Goodman, headphones on. Done with work, I sort through photographs, on the computer and in the shoebox, as I always do for my mother. It's the easiest way of showing her who we are, how we live, and what she's missed. She hasn't been back since I was born here, the year they lived in Beverly. Eighteen months after my birth, she was summoned back to Scotland to care for her dying mother. She never returned.

After she left us, father always spoke about her calmly, while making it perfectly clear he had no intention of seeing her again. He never remarried. He raised me alone. I've visited her every summer since I was seven. Before that, for five years, I didn't see her at all.

When my father – her husband – died, she sent a card.

Of course, since Sheila 2 signed up with the Marines and left home four years ago, we don't take many pictures. Here's one of Woodrow, our dachshund, now happily sporting with the half dozen other dogs our pet-sitter's putting up. Here's one Sheila sent us for Christmas, showing her in front of a tank somewhere outside Basra. When she reenlisted last spring we couldn't believe it. We're pacifists, Gibbs and I. We've seen the photos of what she did. I don't know how to talk about it.

And I know I won't pack those for Mother.

By the time I get to bed, Gibbs is snoring so loud I start wishing a bug would nest in my ear.

I lie straight, hands to the sides, eyes fixed on the ceiling, and count my breaths.

I think back to the last time I saw my daughter, two years ago. Before returning for her second tour of duty, Sheila had a couple of months. One she spent in New York with friends – or that's what she said. And one with us. We noticed nothing unusual. She hadn't done anything incriminating yet – and she was always scarily self-contained. She didn't speak much as a child, and when she went to school she practically stopped talking altogether.

"Selective mutism" they called it. Medications and therapies helped her survive without attending a special school, but just barely. When Sheila was first diagnosed we were stunned, partly because words were never something Gibbs or I had trouble with. She simply couldn't speak in public.

Her first grade teacher was the one who summoned us. We met in the principal's office and listened while she explained how she'd tried coaxing and cajoling, doling out treats and praise without even winning a smile from Sheila, never mind an answer. Gibbs and I looked at the teacher apologetically.

What else do I remember that might give a clue? I've done this inventory a thousand times.

As a girl she saw the movie *Twister* and for a long time afterwards she insisted she wanted to be a storm chaser. She herself was anything but tempestuous. Yet she learned to make her presence felt in ways that didn't require speech. She wanted to please. That was her forte. Not the sharpest pencil, but always at hand. Especially for the tedious chores, the ones no one wanted to do, like scrubbing dog pee out of the carpet. Because she rarely talked, you could count on her to be quiet, efficient, and focused. At family gatherings she became the official dishwasher. Even the several times she visited my mother with me, she was first at the sink, first to walk Mother's beagle Walter Scott, the only one offering to make someone else's bed. As I said, she aimed to please.

School was a misery for her. That was the most normal thing about her. She did, in her last years there, find a couple of friends with whom she shared interests, even if they were far from the ones we urged on her. They were the kind of kids I know too well from my own years of teaching: sullen-eyed boys who scorn skateboards, dress ghetto, and occasionally make the local paper for some act of minor vandalism. The girls wear black, with piercings everywhere, and text each other during class. When Sheila convinced Gibbs to let her join the local gun club, we all but celebrated her move toward the mainstream. We never let her buy a gun, of course: would never have one in the house under any circumstances; but she had friends whose parents felt differently, and on weekends she went with them for target practice at a range outside town. Like a lot of teenagers, she was a fan of those gross movies showing people – usually young women – being dismembered by madmen in face masks. She handed me one called *Tablesaw* and urged me to watch it. She said it was a very moral film. I couldn't get over the box cover, never mind put it on. Yet millions of kids love this stuff.

This last time, finally home with us after a month of doing who knows what in New York, she rented only comedies. We watched *Meet the Fockers, The 40-Year-Old Virgin,* and old Marx Brothers films. We went to Plum Island, tramped the Joppa flats, and drove deep into the bird sanctuary. She pointed out it was a late mating season for the redwinged blackbirds.

I could tell she was holding herself close. She wasn't talking much, even for her. I asked if she was still taking her medication. She nodded absently.

She was working through something.

"I'm your mother, pumpkin nose," I said.

She nodded, forcing a half smile.

Gibbs is suddenly so quiet I prod him to make sure he's still alive. It's like I pressed a button. The snoring resumes.

I shut my eyes, but that can't stop my mind from racing. I see Sheila clearly, as though she were projected on my lids. I'm tempted to tell the figment to redo her eye makeup. I used to say that kind of thing, too often. It was one of the few things that made her angry, as though she could intuit what I'd never say.

The beauty gene in our family has been going steadily

south for several generations. My grandmother was an actress who performed before Queen Victoria. Judging by photographs my father – an engineer at Polaroid – took of my mother, she was, in her day, pretty smashing herself. I, alas, took after my father, who was plain as a donut. The children Gibbs and I produced continued this downward trajectory.

Sheila 2 wasn't cute, which made things harder. She's big-boned, with a large head, and nose, and big teeth. See her, you think horse. I'm just being honest. It's one of my flaws.

Her impulse to please was her way of compensating, I'm sure, and, unfortunately it extended to men. She may not have had witty banter and flashing looks to distract them, but I imagine she made any object of her affection feel like a king. That counts for more than we'd like to think. She gave up at least one child that I know of.

They say she probably inherited my anxiety. I was a fretful child, a hormonal adolescent, yet I'm not a nervous adult. Teaching led me out of that trap. Sheila wasn't so lucky. A part of the brain that processes threats was hyperactive in her. So they said. To which I answer: Sirs, the world is full of threats. Sometimes you're right to be anxious.

But mine didn't drive me to do what she did.

I get up and go to the bathroom where the porcelain angel nightlight illumines my reflection as I pass the mirror. I look away too late. Improbable as it sounds, I realize how much of myself I actually see in her.

I put the toilet seat down.

Suspicion inevitably falls on the parents. It's what I think when reading such a story in the papers.

People assume it's about sex. Was she abused? Did

Gibbs or I do something to her when she was an infant? I caught that question in many a neighbor's eye. Only Helen from across the street said she was sorry about Sheila. Others let their thoughts race by unchecked, for all to see. But there was nothing covert going on around our house sexually – unless, of course, it was so secret I missed it myself. Not impossible, I'll grant. And that's part of the poison: you begin to doubt the details of your own daily life, the one you've been living. Like someone else knows better what you've done, and what you haven't.

Washing my hands, I keep my head down so as not to look into the mirror again. When I reach for the towel, I find it on the floor. Gibbs, Gibbs, I think before recalling I'd used the bathroom last.

Besides, sex isn't the only reason people go bad. Sometimes the causes lie elsewhere entirely.

Helen says there's always another side.

But what other side could there be?

They captured them, chained them, stripped them. And that was only the beginning.

Plus they took photos.

The night is so clear, Venus looks nearer than Newark. The giant beech in full summer leaf flippers the air like a school of fish. Any moment it might zip away. I remember once when both the kids were small we took them on a whale watch in a glass-bottom boat where you could see the underwater neighborhoods, each different from the rest. Sheila stretched out on the floor and pressed her face to the glass, losing herself so utterly in that world that when the cry of "whale" came we had to drag her up to the deck so she could see what the rest of us were marveling at, and not just what she dreamed alone. Initially sulky, she watched the whales leap and spew and she began to smile and wave with the rest of the kids. When she smiled at you, the universe felt right. The moment they were gone, she raced back into the glass belly of the boat.

Something stirs in the junipers, then two skunks emerge and waddle toward the compost pile. The sight of them is strangely comforting.

This time, when I crawl between the sheets, Gibbs is quiet. In minutes I'm asleep.

The next morning, I wake up oddly excited and stretch out sideways on the empty bed, smiling. It almost feels like Christmas. I dreamed the President's wife was coming for lunch. She heard I needed help. It was thrilling. Everyone was there: both my parents, Gibbs, our kids. The problem was cleaning the house, which kept changing as I approached it: one minute it was like our current home, then like the apartment in New York, then my childhood home with the blue shutters. I tried keeping my eyes closed, the better to fondle the dream's details, and didn't notice as, bit by bit, they turned into something else entirely, as my mind drifted to thoughts of what we'd never see – the families of the victims. What were they thinking now, those mothers and daughters of the people our daughter killed? Were they moving ahead with their lives? Could I?

A bolt of inspiration drives me out of bed. I stumble to the bathroom. What if we made it our life's work to help the victims' families? It might not even cost that much, I think, reaching again for the towel. It might help us all.

This morning everything is quiet. I'm barely out of bed when my back insists I lie down on the floor. I obey.

Gibbs is already out; all the neighbors are away (it's August); the house is utterly still.

The floor is covered with a thick beige carpet and I stretch out my arms and legs as far as they'll go. This is what it's like to be dead, I think. Once it arrives, the thought refuses to leave. What it's like to be dead! A sneak preview. Coming attractions. You lie there and you don't move and you're aware of everything that's going on around you, but it's not about you anymore. Finally it's just about them.

I shut my eyes and imagine this room without me.

The bed with the brass headboard; the giant spirit catcher from Santa Fe on one wall; the halogen torchiere; the teak dresser with the row of photographs, including one of Zack and the two Sheilas on the Royal Mile in Edinburgh, just below the castle, taken hours before Zack sprained his ankle on the nighttime Jekyll and Hyde tour; next to it stands my parents' wedding photo in a double frame with one of Gibbs and me. The two couples eye each other warily, as though half-conscious that they share more than they know.

Nothing left but the stuff, no me to dust or dream.

Not so bad, in the end. That exhausting business of being one's self over. Nothing left to resent or grieve. Just nothing, nothing at all.

I cross my arms over my chest and squeeze my forearms. Gradually my breathing slows.

Today we fly to San Diego. Tomorrow we rent a car and drive to Miramar, where the prison is. I've never been to California. At the last minute we decided to take a few days in San Francisco. Gibbs found a reasonable place in the Haight. I've wanted to see it ever since junior high, when I first heard about the summer of love. I was a Grateful Dead fan then. We also bought trip insurance, in case we need to cancel Scotland. In case my daughter needs me.

It's strange to think my mother doesn't. She's glad to see

me, yet she gets along just fine alone. I tried ushering her to Skype, Gibbs had a laptop ready, but she refused. Why, she asked? You young people have a mania for staying in touch. We didn't do that in my day. We saw the person we were with. We saw the trees that grew around us. We ate food from our neighbors' fields, the sheep they fattened. And we lived in the house where we were born. This will sound boring to you, but for me there's more variety in a morning's work in the garden than I could imagine seeing on the dearest safari.

Your generation has lost touch with solitude, she says to me often.

I'm toweling myself dry in the bedroom, clothes laid out on the quilt, when Gibbs comes in holding a bottle of eardrops. His pained face suggests the colony is growing. He's wearing the Hush Puppies I hate and a pink shirt with the collar buttoned. I frown.

"Zack phoned while you were in the shower."

"And?"

"He apologized. Said he has something he wants us to bring out to Sheila."

"Think we'll be allowed to give her anything?"

"I doubt it."

"Did he say what it was?"

Gibbs shook his head.

It occurs to me that for a couple of talkers, Gibbs and I didn't do much of a job communicating what we felt to our kids.

"I went out to get this." He holds up the eardrops.

I nod. I stare at Gibbs for so long he starts to fade, until I can hardly tell he's there.

My daughter wanted to please the world. Why? She wanted to be liked because she felt so alone. She needed others' approval because we couldn't offer enough.

Instead she tried to please the President and his awful men. They do what they do and never look back. They plant their ideas in people. Good people, rich soil. Then they water them with words. Big words, luscious words: God, service, country, patriot, hero. Empty words; cheap talk. They know they're lying. The words mean nothing in their mouths. But they pour them like rain on innocent ground. They bewildered my daughter. She grew like a plant groping for light, twisted and turned as they'd have her, until this. And then the light went out. And they wanted nothing to do with what they had made.

Like houseflies in crickets, they eat us alive.

Where will I, who, truth be told, never seemed to please anyone either – except maybe Gibbs – now find comfort? My daughter needs me. What can I say to you, daughter?

I can still pray, and I do. That my father taught me and it's no small thing. Who am I to throw stones? The only thing ... I wonder sometimes if prayer doesn't reinforce what it intends to relieve. I mean our solitude, since our joys are invariably shared. Count them with me: birthdays, kisses, real kisses, that first burn of love – I've known that burn, the joy of it, and I want you to know it, daughter. To feel it yourself. Understand me: I accept the blame. For you. I do. I lied – to you, to Gibbs, to myself, to everyone. I was never in love with the good man I married. You must have felt it. But I know what love demands, and I want you to know it too. What you've done is so hard, and real, and some part of it will go on forever. The amends we make we will keep making for just as long. Yet, despite everything, I promise you one day you will be invited to love. Accept that invitation. When the time comes, walk with us.

Embodiment

My first week at college, the long-haired brunette who lived down the hall invited me to see *La Strada*. A breathless, feminist Jew from Riverdale, she owned lashes thick as brushes and opinions like fire. We'd met the night before. There'd been a shooting in our dorm. At two in the morning we heard what sounded like an explosion. Zoe and I fled our respective rooms to find Hiram Weatherbee, comically tall, with unnervingly white hair pulled back in a ponytail, standing in the common area with blood geysering from his right shoulder. He looked like an overgrown child who'd just burned himself on a match. Rumor was he dealt; we assumed a deal gone south. The next day we learned that his male lover decided the easiest way to break up was to shoot.

Others quickly arrived on the scene. By then Zoe and I had begun talking. She wailed on Reagan and rhapsodized about her water pipe. She quoted Trotsky and made fun of Tolstoy, and confessed she'd had two abortions. Her full lips looked like they longed to be bloodied, abused in a twisted love-fest.

La Strada was the college's midnight movie the next night.

At eleven, I knocked on her door.

Enter, she said.

Zoe sat cross-legged on her bed, gray sweatpants hiked to her knees, soulful orange halter hardly hiding her breasts. She smiled up at me through long black bangs and patted the sheet beside her.

I sank down, suddenly unsteady.

A cello grinned in the corner.

You have entered the sanctum, she said; at which point I realized she was stoned.

I am here, I echoed. I'd never smoked pot; nor had I ever been close to a stoned stone-cold fox.

Sensing my confusion, Zoe leant forward and kissed me.

*

So let me ask you: What's the purpose of embodiment?

Here we are, you and I, strangers linked only by words on a page, or more likely a screen. Who knows if I'm still alive? You, presumably, are. You may be rosy and robust, or thin and anxious. Doesn't matter. Maybe you're bedridden, or in a wheelchair. You may be on life-support. Or perhaps – and why not? – you're that rare bird, a young person who reads, because you too want some clue about what's coming. One thing for sure: you have a body. You are embodied. So obvious it sounds dumb, I know, but since it's so obvious, let me ask you: Why? To what end? Why have you been embodied?

As soon as Pamela arrived, we began fucking like crazy. You may think that sordid, given our age difference (eighteen; forty), baby asleep in the stroller, but sometimes sordidness is what's called for. I don't say this lightly. A dog-eared copy of my life is the only book I own now, and with the end in sight I'll turn the pages at my own pace, thank you very much.

I didn't ask her to bring the kid.

My new girlfriend, Zoe, briefly mentioned above, was studying in the room down the hall.

Betrayal was my guiding light.

I was eighteen; Pamela was forty; the child belonged to her sister.

It's not my end in sight.

Later, Pamela said: You love powerlessness too much. You want power then you should love money and pussy but you want just one out of two, which won't cut it.

When she saw that didn't land, she added:

The idea of a working-class literature is ridiculous – because the working classes don't read books. They watch wrestling on TV.

She sat up on the single bed with her shirt off and waited.

They also beat their wives, I pointed out. They beat each other. They beat off. That's the working classes for you.

She was too embarrassed to answer.

She'd said it because she felt guilty. She called attention to my class to make herself feel better about sleeping with me, a student from her class. Then the baby started crying.

Dorm life!

*

Zoe's kiss hangs in the air, and I'm beginning to suspect we'll never see the next few scenes, where we bounce about on the bed, dry-humping until nearly midnight, then race across campus so as not to miss *La Strada*, which we loved. We saw it again after we moved to New York together. Then again two years later, at the Bleecker, as we were breaking up.

It was *our* movie.

When Zoe found out I was also sleeping with Pamela, her faculty advisor in Women's Studies, as well as my Chaucer professor, she was, initially, excited. She couldn't think of anyone for a quartet, so she proposed a trio.

One afternoon the two of us, wearing only towels, greeted Pamela, the great authority on "The Nun's Priest's Tale", who expected me alone.

A toga party! Pamela giggled and shut the door behind her. She liked visiting my dorm. She said her nosey neighbors would notice if I came around her house while her husband was at work. Welcome to Ohio! They didn't know he cheated on her with everyone at the office, including the men. The heart has its reasons. On the other hand, she didn't mind other students wondering what was up. Such arrangements were not yet unusual. At that point Zoe and I had been together less than two months. Christmas was approaching. Everyone was feeling festive, and randy.

After Zoe and I broke up, we both stayed in New York. She became a prosecutor and now lives with a woman who plays second violin in the Philharmonic. I became an actor. I played Off-Broadway, Off-Off-Broadway, and Nowhere in Sight of Broadway. Pamela was right. About money, pussy, power.

*

The woman I'm with now is none of the above. Yet, truth be told, didn't she send all of them to me? Wasn't each her gift, her curse?

My mother is in the next room, dying.

I move restlessly through the cramped, curtained quarters in which I grew up, where she raised me. Herself. Alone. My own personal engineer of human souls. Not just mine. My mother gave herself to whatever needed her:

people, animals, objects – chachkas of every stripe, men in all colors. Now I water her plants – the ivies, violets; spiders spinning webs for decades in her shadow. She used to talk to them, urging me to do the same. "Go on," she'd say. "They hear every word."

I bet they're pining for her now.

Can't bring myself to do it, though.

Her name kept changing, but it was always you, Mother, wasn't it? I think this while lying in my boyhood bed, below a calendar announcing 1968. Year of my birth; year of the assassins. She refused to take it down, no matter how often I asked.

Each visit, I tried losing pieces of the past surrounding her – I hoped in time to clear away enough to see her as she really is.

All these years I've lived in New York, just twenty miles north, I rarely saw my mother, which must have been hard for her. She was alone a lot. Her boyfriends were damaged men who rarely looked me in the eye and never stayed. But I was always busy, working, waitering, answering phones in a hospital or doing graphic design for a website. Evenings, there were the plays. My career began on a high note: my first time out, in a play by David Rabe, I was nominated for an Obie. Now I practically live here, in my old hometown in Jersey, from which I fled, hair on fire, twenty years ago. If things don't change soon I'll have to sublet my studio back in the city.

*

Since she left, thirteen months ago, my wife's name has rarely crossed my lips. It's just a thing that happened. We sat beside each other on a flight, through turbulence and highs that swore eternity but lied. Was she the first to go? Was I? Irrelevant, thanks to mother. Timing couldn't have been better. Again she's saved me. Instead of licking my wounds, I've come to ease her passage.

What made it even easier was the accident. A few weeks after my wife left I was performing in *Nor Are We Out of It* at the Triangle. The production had been cursed from the start. Maybe it was the premise – New York as Dante's Hell – or the interactive side of it. Audiences were handed iPads in place of programs and invited to propose new torments for the sinners, many of whom worked in finance – as did much of our audience. In any case, that first week I tripped descending a stairway into a cauldron of black ice and wound up with a fractured tibia. Now Mom and I could play invalid together.

My first weeks here I whirled with the motes in a twilight of mother's medications, insurance forms, and piles of junk. Late Pompeian, cloaked in ash. Like nature, mother abhors a vacuum cleaner. Old lamps, decades of Christmas ornaments in boxes, vases of crumbling flowers, fraying pillows, stacks of magazines and newspapers. Paperweights embedded with beetles, purple eyeglasses, broken pencils, yellowed phone books, jars empty and full. Someone's medals from WWI. Photographs, photographs. The collective weight of the memories threatened to bury me, so I began this journal. When she's gone I'll have it to show who's been here.

O but the stuff, the stuff. Xanadu, by Walmart. Makes me glad I travel light.

Can I at least get rid of the lamp? I asked.

Don't touch that lamp, she said.

Why not? It doesn't work.

I don't remember. It doesn't matter. Just don't touch it.

And if mother really is out of it, how can you tell, honestly, given the state of the Union, what passes for normal, given the world?

*

La Strada.

What?

It's young Fellini, Mother!

We're in the living room, watching a DVD. Mother's in her wheelchair, nuzzling her blanket. I'm about to burn a hole in the couch with my cigarette, I'm that relaxed, feet on a pillow.

The Road, Mother says. I've walked that road. Lotta potholes in it. Turn up the volume, I can't hear.

It's in Italian, I say. Read the subtitles.

I don't see so good no more.

She said to me once about herself: When I came into the world I saw that everything the world needed, it already had – but one. I was superfluous, except as myself.

As herself, she was unprecedented.

What's it about? Mother asks.

I sit up and look at her. Her fine features have collapsed on themselves in the last years and I'm hard pressed to rediscover the shapely face that once seemed born to taunt the men who couldn't stay away – until, at some point, the tables turned, and in her desperation to find a man, she willingly abased herself in ways no son could bear to see, or rehearse. I bore it by not looking. It was her life, her self.

The wounded slyness round the eyes and lips, below the shriveled folds, will testify.

The road, I replied. You said it yourself.

What about the road?

It's hard, it's long, and one day it's over, I say, lighting another cigarette.

Oh, there's more to it than that. Her voice is a whisper.

There's music, I offer.

Music, she nods. And people. You meet good people on the road.

Silence.

*

After the movie, I put her to bed then sit down to sift through pictures of the good people she met along the way. She keeps her photographs in shoe boxes stacked in her closet. In most cases the faces are as strange to me as my own is rapidly becoming.

Then there's the story mother has told over and over, for which there is no photo. My grandfather, her father, sits at one end of a very large waiting room, in a wooden chair that's too small, like a schoolboy anticipating the principal. At the other end, behind an ugly brown desk, looms a secretary, head buried in a ledger. Portraits of dour-faced men adorn the walls, a red star in the center of their uniform brown caps.

It's cold. The heat's not worked in days. A glass of water on the secretary's desk has turned to ice. My grandfather relights his pipe for something warm to wrap his fingers around. Suddenly there's a noise at the other end of the room. The floor behind the door creaks. My grandfather swallows. He begins to rise, so that by the time the door opens my grandfather is on his feet and moving.

Into the room marches Tolstoy.

Telling me that story made mother feel part of history. Images of people no one else remembers are leaving her body and entering mine. When she's gone, they'll be mine alone. Is that the meaning of embodiment?

Thinking about it directly, I suspect it's about sex. Sure, love. Sure, there's love – but do you need embodiment for that? Besides, the kind of sex I'm talking about is bigger than love. Maybe sex isn't the right word anymore; maybe it never was. Then, what?

Personally, I want to be remembered as a dog whose tongue was bigger than his bark.

*

To save money, mother always bought our shoes on sale. Sizes were approximate. Over years of wearing penny loafers one size too small, I told myself, I was like a Chinese bride, bound for better things. I couldn't bear to make my mother feel bad. How is it none of these stories are about her?

I'm the one who's forty now. Mother will be seventy-eight next month. If she lives.

At the giant Shop Rite I buy hummus, tomatoes, and boxes of Depends. I walk down the aisles like a tourist lost on Mars. The death toll in Haiti's earthquake hovers around 200,000. Though I stroll amid a hundred thousand different food items, there are no smells. While studying the kinds of chips available (vegetable, tortilla, nachos, potato, pita, bagel) I try to imagine my grandfather's conversation with the great Russian writer. An interview with Tolstoy! For years I've mulled the meaning of this legendary encounter.

What would I ask him, if the chance were mine?

Okay: Do you wish you'd stayed home, Tolstoy?

Is it really better never to have been born? (I know you didn't say that, but it gets to the heart of the matter, doesn't it?)

If the kingdom of God is within, what happens to that real estate when we die?

Finally, what was it with all those sweaty little moustaches on your women?

Great men know nothing. That they know.

*

At dinner I ask mother to tell me what she thinks grandfather asked Tolstoy.

Tolstoy? Her eyes widen. Today her face looks smaller than ever, so tiny I could fit it into one of those lockets she has on her bureau.

You know, the big waiting room, the secretary, the frozen water ...

Oh, *that* story. But that wasn't Tolstoy.

What do you mean? For years you repeated that story. *Tolstoy marches into the room* it always ended.

You're forgetting. It wasn't Tolstoy. It was Trotsky.

Trotsky?

She's right. I remember now. The borscht cools in my spoon: golden globules of fat in purple water swell. I changed the name in my mind because I had no questions for Trotsky.

*

I once took a blind woman by the elbow and helped her navigate a busy corner at rush hour, only to find when we reached the other side that she'd never intended to cross. "You fucking people think you know everything," she said. So I left her there, cursing and disoriented, on the wrong side of the street, and retreated to wherever it was I also had no wish to be going. Such was my life back then. But sometimes things do work out, or can, in the imagination.

So I imagine Tolstoy entering the room. Somehow his deep-fisted eyes found space for nearly sixty years of marriage, the birth of thirteen kids, then the death of five, his long-suffering genius of a wife, the sycophants and fans who gathered around him, as well as the peasants and horses he loved, because the nothing they have is all he wants. He understands what I'm going through, sees the ruins of a marriage smoldering behind me, together with the textures of my present tense: the quilted miseries of mothers and sons. He forgives nothing – that's not his job, and maybe he no longer judges. Besides, it's not forgiveness I want – and certainly not sermons about the world to come, or lectures about art. The hell with my ex and how my grasping drove her ever further south, back to her home and her people. The hell, too, with my mother, who's had her own life, and can't possibly want mine – can she? I'll settle for a simple wink of recognition from the great man, some hint that he too knows.

Tolstoy says nothing, of course. But what I feel from him across the room is a sweet, fraternal pity. Without a word, he lets me know he always knew what science only recently confirmed – that even a rat, when he sees one of his own kind in a cage, will do everything he can to free him.

A cage of my own making, sure, made of age and money, or rather its absence, and the feeling that I'm bound to replay the same dumbshow over and again, forever the man who loved women but not a woman – like my mother and her men, I suppose – until one day I wake up to find myself in a rooming house in New Orleans with a half-pulled shade and an empty bottle of Wild Turkey on the table. (Note to self: try out for a Tennessee Williams play.) Once, finding myself in such a mood, I might have ditched everything and hit the road – for Greece, or London, or Vermont, to my friend Tom's place in the Northeast Kingdom. I can't do that now. "Responsibilities." My cage. My rage.

*

Years after I graduated college, one of my old prof Pamela's student-lovers tired of her pedagogy and reported her to the administration. It was a time of national penance, triggered by the president's blue dress or something equally déclassé. The shame was too much. Pamela quit teaching, left Ohio, and eventually disappeared. I'd look her up periodically on Lexis-Nexis, but the last thing I ever found was an article about Wilde's *De Profundis,* from November 20__.

Then, one morning about a year ago, soon after I discovered my wife was leaving me for her boss at the hospital, I was walking down Bleecker Street, on my way to see my therapist. It was a cold December day and everyone was bundled up like Siberian exiles. I was about to turn the corner when I saw her standing at the light across the street. Her hair was silver. She wore a stylish scarf and her nose was pierced. Otherwise she looked exactly the same. She raised her arm. I thought maybe she'd spotted me. As I debated whether to call out to her, the light changed. "Pamela," I shouted.

A cab drove up and she was about to get in when she must have seen me flapping my arms in her direction. She stopped, stared as I ran toward her, and waved the cab off.

She stood on the corner, stiff as a sergeant, hands by her sides. When I reached her, huffing and sweating, she stared at me without any sign of recognition.

"Pamela," I said.

She narrowed her eyes. Her face had hardened considerably. The years had flattened her cheeks and compressed her nose, leaving her looking vulpine and harsh.

"Do I know you?" she asked, struggling to see across distances to those six months two decades ago when our bodies tangled like eels in a stew.

"You," she said. "I can't believe they let you live."

But that's how it is with embodiment.

The Man Who Would Not Bow

The Chronology of a Crime: St Petersburg, 1881-1887

ALEXANDER RECALLED MINNIE'S face the moment his father, the emperor, was carried into the palace, after the bomb shredded his leg. The sole of his left foot flapped loose, dangling like a dog's tongue, drooling blood on the marble. Minnie bit her finger to keep from crying out. Alexander pressed his forehead to her shoulder, inhaled her perfume, shut his eyes. *Rallet*: the French were geniuses with scent.

He could no longer dream. That part of life was over. Years later, when his private train was derailed by anarchists, Tsar Alexander propped the car's ceiling on his shoulders while his wife and children crawled out the window. That car freighted his back the rest of his days, and he could never unload it. His empire, meanwhile, was also running off the tracks. Threats against the royal couple forced them to flee St Petersburg for the Gatchina Palace. Thirty miles outside the city, its nine hundred rooms became home for the next thirteen years. Even there they weren't safe. A plot to assassinate them during mass was foiled, and the five conspirators, who planned to hide their dynamite inside hollowed-out bibles, hung. Among them the older brother of the man who later called himself Lenin.

Before turning revolutionary, Lenin's brother, Alexander, had been an aspiring biologist. Defending himself in court, he declared: "Terror is our answer to the violence of the state."

On hearing of his brother's execution, the seventeen-year-old Lenin said, "I'll make them pay for this." And so, in time, he did.

1918

1

By the time Mykola left the barbershop off Nevsky Prospect and turned into the newly renamed *Square of the Uprising*, the sun had nearly burned away the morning mist. Only a wreath of cloud crowned the cupola of Our Lady of the Sign.

What rose up that morning was June's potpourri of steaming horseshit and mud. It had taken the revolution more than a decade to topple the monarchy, yet the statue of Tsar Alexander astride his horse still dominated the square, reminding people of the yoke from which they'd lately been liberated.

Compact, muscled as a muzhik, and sporting a goatee like the leader's, Mykola dropped a fistful of kopeks into the cap of a blind beggar sitting on the curb. The revolution still had a ways to go.

The revolution which began over borscht. Bowls of it, laced with rotten meat, were served to the crew of the Battleship Potemkin. The last straw. The men mutinied, murdering their captain, and sailed for the port of Odessa. The sailors' rebellion sparked a round of strikes and work-stoppages across the empire. Mykola had been there from the start, marching with Father Gapon on the Winter Palace in 1905.

Since then, Mykola's differences with his comrades had seen him slide into his current role as aide to the Commissioner of the Central Telephone Station in St Petersburg, to whose office he now hurried. Word had arrived about their next assignment. They were to transfer the Tsar and his family back to Moscow. Mykola was to accompany the Commissioner as an assistant to the chief telegraph operator communicating with the Kremlin.

*

Living in the antique luxury of the old governor's mansion in Tobolsk, the city to which he himself had exiled countless revolutionaries, the Tsar recalled the day he awoke as simply Nicholas Romanov again, with no empire to drag him down. The former royal family were fed the same bland rations as their guards: no more butter or coffee, no more sweets. And, not long after that, the group was ordered to prepare to move again, this time to Moscow.

The thaw had set in and the rains would not relent. Mud painted tires; it coated boots and wagon wheels and the naked feet of the millions of men, women, and children marching from one town to the next to escape the violence. It crusted hearts. The civil war was at its pitch.

Having picked up their illustrious cargo, which they referred to as “the baggage”, the Commissioner and Mykola were blocked on their way to the capital by Ural Bolsheviks who diverted the convoy to Ekaterinburg, on the border between Europe and Asia. There the royals bunkered in a building dubbed *The House of Special Purpose.*

The Commissioner and Mykola recognized immediately what this spelled for “the baggage”.

“A disaster,” moaned the Commissioner, who’d hoped to keep the royal family safe, even as he was eager to return to his own. Anyway, what could he do? It was out of his hands, and the holidays were approaching. He rushed off to Moscow leaving Mykola in charge of “the baggage”. “Take notes,” he instructed.

Mykola never talked about this period in his life; it was like he’d dreamed it, like it had been a movie watched through the smoke of a burning theatre where no one had bothered to cry “fire!” He knew the games his comrades played. He understood the letters “smuggled” to the Tsar were snares, bait for “evidence” to justify the preordained.

The local party chief himself raced to Moscow to address the Central Committee. Lenin, remembering what Nicholas’ father had done to his brother, tipped his head back and nodded.

On July 16, the commandant of the *House of Special Purpose* was told the time had come. He composed a final telegram to Moscow, asking that the order of execution be confirmed. Unwilling to deliver it, Mykola handed off to a subordinate. He himself slipped in for a last chat with the Tsar.

*

The room's ceiling sagged, the children were sniffling, and Alexandra looked tellingly grim. What was it like for them, moving from palace to prison? How did Nicholas explain this to his girls? Mykola heard from others there were screams at night. He saw how the girls and women quaked when he entered, and even though the Tsar would immediately step up to distract his attention, he noticed the buttons missing from blouses badly mended, the scratch marks on the girls' pale faces, their sunken, shadowed eyes.

Turned out the Tsar and he were both ardent stamp collectors. The hobby had recently taken Europe by storm. The tiny, perforated squares – like static screens – gave structure to men's daydreams of a wider world. Cousin George of England presided over the Royal Philatelic Society. The self-same cousin had offered Nicholas and his family shelter, before taking the advice of his ministers and recanting.

Mykola heard the rare Mauritius postage stamp was coming up for auction. Maybe the tsar would like to bid?

Nicholas, whose favorite pastime had been shooting birds, sighed and glanced forlornly at his captor. Funny. Killing small animals was a passion he'd shared with the late Archduke, Franz Ferdinand, who had also been assassinated. Birds were angels. The tsar was not the fool he often seemed. The future was not hard to read: it lay like a seed, like bird seed, in the present moment.

He rose, eyes down. The toe of his boot sketched a circle in the carpet. Finally he looked up. As the men shook hands, Mykola saw Alexei, the hemophiliac heir, drag his index finger across his own throat and drop his neck like it had been slit.

Realizing the inappropriateness of his remark but unsure of what else to say, Mykola pulled his coat tight and left the room. He cast a worried glance over his shoulder as the guard locked the door behind him.

*

The executioners calmed themselves by drinking. No one knew who'd win this bloody civil war. Killing an emperor and his family – Alexandra, Maria, Anastasia, Tatiana, Olga, and the heir apparent, Alexei – wasn't work for amateurs. Alive, they would forever stain the state's legitimacy. But the business needed to be done discreetly, late, and in the dark, without alarming the neighbors. Nothing civil in a civil war.

The royal family, along with their entourage, were wakened near midnight and told to dress. They were to be moved again, away from the front. Led to the basement – ostensibly to escape into a truck at the back of the house – the family suspected the truth. They looked at one another and said nothing. The commandant asked them to huddle together. The reds wanted a group portrait to show the world the royals were healthy and intact. Alexandra requested chairs for herself and Alexei, which were quickly brought, along with a third, for the Tsar.

Disarmed by the promise of a photographer, the family were surprised when a dozen members of the secret police arrived, brandishing pistols, lurching drunkenly in the tight quarters. The Tsar rose up to ask a question and at that moment the commandant ordered his men to fire. Twenty minutes and over seventy bullets later, the basement was filled with blinding smoke, acrid and sour. The bodies of the seven royals, along with their maid, a private physician, and another servant, lay scattered across the floor. Naturally, the executioners had botched the job: the children were still alive and had to be finished off with bayonets, while neighbors gathered in the street. The bodies were then frisked for jewels – yielding several pounds of diamonds sewn into the clothing. As they were being carried out on stretchers, one of the children, Anastasia, moaned, and was quickly bayoneted and shot again. Only Alexei's spaniel, Joy, survived the night.

Notebook in hand, Mykola watched the bodies bundled into the trucks. There was no going back. It was a hot July night, and the mosquitoes were thick and merciless. Everyone was sweating. Sweat dripped on the pages of his notebook. All across the neighborhood, roused by gunfire, dogs barked at the sky. Mykola shut his eyes. It was like an invisible hand had seized the book of time and torn it in half. Shredded it. Tossed the pieces into the air. Now night preceded afternoon and morning bled directly into night.

He shoved his notebook into his pocket and stared down at a rosebush trampled by the executioners' boots. This was not what he'd wanted from his revolution. Or was it? What had anybody wanted? A horse screamed in the distance. His eyes dazzled. They died young.

He remembered watching his father die. He'd been working in coal mines outside Luhansk from the age of five and had by forty breathed more crystalline silica and coal dust in the underworld than he'd inhaled clean air above. The family of eight lived in a one-room shack and it was impossible to escape the sound of his coughing. All day and through the night his father coughed until he could no longer breathe at all. The next year, his mother, who'd worked the mines since she was ten, died the same way and Mykola, twelve, was left to care for his five brothers and sisters.

The trucks carrying the bodies roared off. The burial, he later heard, was slowed because the killers brought only one shovel for the dozen drunken gravediggers who paused to grope the tsarina's body, scooping her genitals for diamonds, which they found. They severed fingers to seize rings. In the end, their boss left with 19lbs of glittering rocks. But the grave they dug was too shallow. The crew had to return the next night to drag out the bodies, already decomposing under the sulfuric acid poured on them the night before. They hurled the corpses onto Fiat trucks. On their way to a copper mine, they got stuck in mud. The gravediggers, who'd volunteered in hope of further defiling the royals, dumped "the baggage" in the road. The darkness was like the inside of a velvet glove. The bodies were mutilated yet again and cast into a pit, then layered over, almost casually, with railroad ties. There they remained, undiscovered, for over half a century.

Mykola returned to St Petersburg more depressed than ever. He wasn't ready to write off the revolution just yet, but he worried how all this might end. Still, something certainly had to be done.

2

When did life stop being a gift and become a loan you had to repay? Forty years after Bloody Sunday, Mykola was not resigned. He lived in fury. The "leaders" had made a mess of it! Let others accommodate the lies, others fight for their comforts, which mustn't be infringed on. Mykola refused to play along. He would hold out. Alone, if necessary. The price you paid for staying human. He never respected *their* power. *They* were his former comrades. He scorned the alleged authority of *their* emissaries, and he never feared *them*. He knew that whatever means *they* had were no match for the power of the imagination, and there he excelled far beyond anything *they'd* ever dreamed. He would remake the world and *they* would be changed in the process.

The amount of blood spilt in the intervening decades astonished everyone. One of Mykola's brothers disappeared in the Siberian Gulag. Another was responsible for stripping farmers in the eastern regions around Kirovohrad of their wheat, abetting a famine which led to millions of deaths. In some villages, cannibalism became common: the bodies of the lately dead were sliced up and placed on outdoor tables for sale like cuts of beef at a charcuterie. Mykola registered the losses in comb rows on his wrists, marking two suicide attempts. Both times he changed his mind. He wasn't ready to give up. Then, in the spasm of a paragraph, he fell in love.

He honored his Armenian grandmother by marrying Larissa in the Armenian Church in Lviv, where he'd fled to escape his enemies in the east. Even Lviv couldn't hide a man as combustible as Mykola, who pissed off everyone, enemies and comrades alike, pushing his résumé to the top of everyone's hit list. Friends urged him to leave before "something happened" to his family but he kept shaking his head, his hair gone white, no, no, he wasn't ready to go, this was home, and soon there was a child, Serge, and he needed to know his native land.

Serge was his parents' second child. The first, Theodosia, had been born with foreshortened limbs and eyes that never opened. Mykola blamed himself for her death, for all that his wife had endured because of him.

Then, one night, he found a crow with its neck broken and its eyes plucked out stuffed in his mailbox and he understood the sign and decided that maybe the time had indeed come to move on. He rubbed the mottled top of the dining-room table. He hammered it with his fists. This solid world around him would soon melt into air. His wife said, Don't worry, my sister will take the table, it won't go to waste. Mykola rose and stepped to the window and stared at the street he'd come to know well over the last couple of years: at the Opera House, where he saw Blavatsky's Hamlet, and standing in front of it, the statue of Lenin. What fools they'd been, so young, dreaming of justice while unleashing the resentment of centuries. Never forget: Stalin's favorite novel was *The Patricide*.

3

Once he took flight, Mykola couldn't stop moving. When nowhere is home, anywhere will do, for a time. No roots, no commitment. He traveled with an entourage of relatives – uncles, aunts, cousins. Keeping at least some of the family intact was a point of pride for Mykola, who knew too well what awaited those left behind.

Where to go was the question. No place on earth was eager to welcome these new refugees. They kept looking. They took the midnight train to Prague. At the border, a young Nazi soldier grew suspicious. The family was detained. Everyone was searched head to toe, then sent to a work camp where they remained until Mykola succeeded in bribing the guards. Bribery had become an art, a spiritual discipline, but you had to make your resources last. So their odyssey began: from Prague they moved to Paris, then Lisbon, from there to Casablanca, back to Lisbon, then London. Having exhausted the hemisphere, they finally shipped off to South America.

Then came a decade of wandering below the equator. Dogged by bad timing, it seemed every country they visited soon went up in flames: Argentina, Chile, Peru, Colombia ... And everywhere new light, new mountains, new people. Only mosquitoes and the philosophy of revolution stayed the same: left versus right; on one side, the military guarding elites; the dispossessed stockpiling weapons on the other. As a boy, Serge wondered how it was that men kept repeating their mistakes time and again.

An activist to the core, that was his father Mykola. His activities bore fruit, though they rarely matched the seeds he thought he'd planted – because none of us ever really understands the consequences of our actions.

From the start, Serge felt himself at the mercy of his father's feuds, which didn't end when the family left Europe. Everywhere they went, from Tierra del Fuego to Montivedeo to Santiago, Mykola discovered enemies. No neighborhood was ever quite *gemutlichkeit*. There was always some right-wing bastard hiding in the weeds, a genocidal Stalinist skulking in the corner bar.

Serge's childhood memories were a blur of impressions. He remembered a train whistle, a plume of steam, and a little girl's severed head by the side of the road. Men, many men. Uniforms. Guns. And the voices spoke German or Russian, Portuguese or Spanish. A few words of English. There was the man with a chalk-white face wearing a necklace of thumbs, a head full of hair set ablaze like a torch, then nothing until that whale alongside the boat which winked at him before diving from sight; later, an albatross on deck after midnight while he shivered under the canvas of the lifeboat, snuggled next to naughty little Sue. Later still, the gossip of squirrels in the park, and that black cat curled in the rear window of the old Buick, hissing as though he was the one to be feared. An old man's voice whispered, "The coffee's too hot."

Years later Serge learned that, because of his father's activities, more than a dozen family members who'd stayed in the old country were either shot or disappeared in the katorgas, the Gulag. Those who left never spoke about it: the dead and disappeared were forgotten, as though they never existed. Only when someone had too much to drink did fragments leak out in stray remarks followed by fiery glances, and then you understood the dead would never go away. They were with you all the time, whether you knew it or not.

Serge heard more than he understood – but he understood enough to know from boyhood on he wanted nothing to do with politics.

4

During the happiest and most stable period of Serge's life, he roomed in a big white house in a village near the sea outside Valparaiso. His first day there, Serge tripped and fell down a flight of stairs, tumbling past wallpaper showing English hunting scenes, all the way to the bottom. He rose unscathed. It was to be a generous and accommodating dwelling. Serge loved the yard and the barn that had once housed carriages and horses. There was a hitching post near the furnace, and horseshoes under the dirt.

Serge was an easy child. His mother often said to him: My, you're so easy! She was the kindest woman. He loved her with all his heart. She read him stories every night: the fables of Aesop, Kipling, and *Lys Mykyta*.

His mother planted rows of apple, peach, and cherry trees around the blue, pink, and white hydrangeas. She also rooted a grape vine and made her own Madeira. Another part of the yard became a productive garden she seeded with corn, tomatoes, squash and various herbs. A mulberry in the side yard twisted past the boy's bedroom window. Serge checked it nightly for monsters said to be trolling the neighborhood.

An uncle raised rabbits in little wooden crates sheathed in wire mesh. He also kept geese and ducks but they were all massacred one summer night by the raccoon whose family had lived in the barn for generations.

Many summer evenings, kids from the neighboring fincas would be playing in the yard, watched over by a clan of raccoons as they licked themselves clean. Once, a neighbor laid a small trap and it caught the mother raccoon. A cousin spotted the wounded creature hobbling, with the trap and chain dragging from her leg, into the barn. A group of kids soon surrounded the building so the racoon couldn't escape. By the time they went in, all that remained were the chain, the trap, and the racoon's hind leg. She was an escape artist, one of them.

No house is without its ghosts and tutelary spirits, but it was Serge's cousin who had the gift of seeing them. The other children envied her. They listened avidly to reports outlining her encounters, which occurred almost daily. These included brushes with a half-woman/half-horse, a floating child in a blue nightgown, and a midget in a stovepipe hat who jumped onto her bed and, doffing his topper with a flourish, bent over and kissed her on the cheek.

*

One evening Serge's father came up to him while he was hunched over math homework. The old man, who'd grown more severe with age, sank slowly down into his chair and plucked at his moustache, the way he always did when he had something serious and important to convey. Serge didn't even look up at first. The poetry of algebra charmed and calmed him with its funny-looking formulas and symbols, a secret language, like the speech of birds. Solving for x had a clarity of purpose that balanced the chaos of daily life.

"Boy," he began, clearing his throat. "I want you to remember something. Your father witnessed the death of God."

Serge sat up straight. Whenever his old man talked like this, it was important not only to pay attention but to make it clear he was listening with all his being, otherwise he might expect a slap to the head. Serge fixated on the bees helicoptering among the bright orange trumpet flowers.

By God, he of course meant *the Tsar*. The collapse of the monarchy ended a dynasty which had ruled Russia for three hundred years. It had been a cruel yet relatively orderly system in which everyone had their place: the nobles lived off the labors of the peasants, whose docility was maintained by brute force. Every so often, a few of the bolder serfs would escape to join the cossacks, a band of freemen whose status as warriors evolved over the centuries until they eventually won a country all their own. But they couldn't hold out against the empire forever. In the end they were crushed and reabsorbed into the system.

"The state, you know," he said, glowering at him through his round, metal-rimmed spectacles, "is a centralizing authority. The failure to centralize successfully is what destroyed the Ancien Regime. France's monarchy couldn't coordinate all aspects of their holdings, you understand, boy?" He didn't, but he could never let him know that. The old man spoke to the boy like an equal, and Serge didn't want to let him down.

"The administration couldn't handle the details, you see. Things slipped through the cracks. Grievances remained unresolved; taxes went unpaid; authorities unappointed. People grew angry at the chaos. These lessons weren't lost on the tsar.

"The reforms he proposed were too little too late. See, boy, history's the frying pan we're sizzling in."

Mykola laughed, frisking the boy's hair. But Serge knew why his father told him these things: he expected the boy to make good on his dreams. Serge bit his lip, and waited for the right moment to light out on his own.

5

While Serge received no formal schooling and earned no degrees, nevertheless, thanks to his father's efforts, by fourteen he spoke four languages fluently and could navigate advanced calculus problems. His mother, meanwhile, made sure her son memorized thousands of lines of poetry by the ubiquitous Shevchenko. She was especially partial to the lachrymose and heroic verses idealizing a grand if violent past.

Serge regarded his father the same way the old man had viewed the Tsar. Some tyrants ruled empires; others had only their families to command. Both shared a faith in the rule of the fist. Vulnerable and dependent, the boy watched and waited.

By twelve, Serge was already working as a bicycle messenger, delivering packages to different parts of Valparaiso. From then on, he managed to find work wherever his father dragged him. Over the years he'd worked as a shepherd, a cowhand, a janitor, a gardener, and a driver of everything from crates of chickens to who knows what. He didn't care what he did, so long as he was able to work.

His moment arrived soon after he turned seventeen. In a *ciudad perdido* in Mexico City he met his bride-to-be. Her name was Yulia. She had been a golden-curled child-actress even before emigrating to Paris accompanied by an aunt with a permanent sniffle. A nineteen-year old divorcée, wheat-blond, sloe-eyed and vivacious, she had a tongue that could cleave a watermelon. She also had no papers. She and her aunt had been robbed by a fellow émigré not long after arriving in the city. All their documents had been stolen. Fortunately, her aunt kept some reserve cash in her underwear, or the pair might have starved. The two women feared they might be stuck in Mexico forever – until Serge. He strode into their lives like El Cid, a Salvador certain he could overcome any obstacle so that the future might in no way resemble the past. "Losing everything," Serge thought, "can be a great blessing." Unfortunately, it can also become a habit.

As to this business of papers – passports, identity cards – who decreed them necessities? Countries were fictions, their borders scribbled in dreams, written in water, and inscribed in blood; holding pens corralling folk like cattle, redefining humans as citizens, dimming their natural radiance until all forgot we are born of light into this world, which is our natural home.

Serge couldn't get over the shame of it. He understood what had made his father so indignant – the lies promoted as laws. He had no trouble getting new papers for Yulia. He used his savings to buy two tickets on a steamer. The poor, sniffling aunt was left behind. Yulia promised to send money and, once they were established, she swore they'd bring her north. They never did. Like Serge's parents, Yulia's aunt was swept away by the relentless tidal pull of war.

Their earliest years, full of struggle, were leavened by intense physical passion. Theirs, Serge believed, was true love. Body and soul met their mate, their other half, just as Plato predicted. They were one on every level, finding peace spooned in a bed, on the floor, or on the bare earth. Didn't matter, so long as they were together. They sang to each other across the room, and their souls hummed in tune when they were forced to walk apart. They never argued. They agreed on everything. They had only one mission: to move east, to New York, where they would find others of their tribe, and there set up lives dedicated to the pursuit of passion, truth, and beauty. They would raise a large family, and never let their love dim or be diminished from the grand, metaphysical thing that it was.

You Never Know For Whom You are Working

1

Yulia's cousin Vera invited the couple to stay with her family in Queens until they could find a place of their own. Yulia took the couch while Serge made himself comfortable on a heap of blankets on the living-room floor. The day after they arrived, they joined the local Orthodox church. That there was such a place was itself a miracle since, back home, most of the bishops and priests had either been murdered or sent into exile. The church was also the place for networking. With help from a fellow parishoner, the couple took a fourth-floor walkup on Manhattan's Lower East Side, where they discovered a host of old-world transplants who gathered nightly at the local bars to swap tales and compare notes, mourn losses, and toast future victories. Serge passed his evenings in the company of men whose patriotic impulses, having no outlet, had never been stronger. They burned to destroy what they'd fled, which had ruined their lives.

One Sunday at coffee hour, following mass, Yulia met Mrs Hrab. The elderly woman, who walked with a cane, told her that Moira O'Connell, for whom the woman had once worked as a cook, needed a nanny.

2

The O'Connells lived in a penthouse on Sutton Place. Breathless and wobbly from trotting the block on ambitious heels, Yulia almost turned back when she saw the uniformed doorman. Uniforms made her knees buckle; her left eye would twitch; she'd begin savagely rubbing a spot on her palm. She lit a cigarette and walked slowly around the corner. She paused before a jewelry-store window displaying a reckless array of diamonds and gold. Her world until recently had been mud and coal and now she was looking at diamonds and gold. Her reflection in the glass gave her a shock. She was beautiful. She remembered her brief but giddy brush with glamour back in Paris as the war was ending – even then, even there. She'd won a part in a crowd scene in *Les Enfants du Paradis*, clandestinely made under the nose of the Nazis, employing Jews and other subversives, and she wouldn't let herself be intimidated by a uniform now. No. She turned back. The doorman bowed slightly and directed her to take the elevator to the top floor.

Yulia understood she was entering another galaxy, which just happened to be accessible by subway. At the door she took two deep breaths and knocked.

3

After a lifetime on the run, Serge suddenly found himself adrift. Having arrived, he was ready to go. The anxieties of their eastward trek were as nothing compared to months of sleepless nights on Vera's floor, waking in the same place, knowing that here was where they'd have to build their home. Both Serge and Yulia felt ragged and uncertain: who were they, really? Why had they come to this city? What did they expect from it? They'd never known a plot of earth to call their own, to call home. They began quarreling. Yulia threatened to leave; Serge stormed from the apartment, staying out all night.

Some nights he walked down Second Avenue over to Broadway, and then down to Battery Park, where he stood along the water's edge and stared out at the lights bouncing along the harbor waters and wondered why he had been born. Watching the waves, he wondered: was there anything constant, anything which couldn't be taken from him?

Serge prowled Manhattan's streets. Scrounging for work at factories and stores around the city, he walked and walked. Despite a syntax spawned by reading Shakespeare and Joyce, Serge's accent turned all his words to rubber. His listeners puzzled, scratched their heads: what was that? He walked and walked. He needed to join a union yet none would have him. In the anti-Communist fifties, Serge was suspect. His father had been a party member, yes, Serge wouldn't deny it. He walked the length of Manhattan, into Harlem and toward the Bronx. Sometimes he found casual day jobs along the way: hauling garbage out of a building that was being demolished, helping a man carry a couch up to the sixth floor. He was open to anything. He walked the East River and the Hudson. In Central Park he stopped to stroke the trees. He envied them their rootedness. He walked and walked. He smoked.

He began hanging out in Washington Square Park, playing chess with other taciturn men, displaced from themselves by events or secret compulsions. When Yulia asked how he spent his days, he lied and said he'd been hunting for work – and the distance between them yawned ever wider. She came home tired, yet with a lift to her voice which told him she was enjoying herself and ready for more. Serge nodded as she outlined her day: beyond the screaming children, the light playing along the river visible from every window, the thick carpet underfoot and the soft sheets on the bed, the toys, the food, the maid and the cook. A life he could never give her.

He thought about his parents. He'd been so eager to leave their home, to get out from under his father's control. Now, in New York, he felt their absence. They had protected him from more than he could possibly have understood at the time. Their bodies had shielded him from monsters. Without their support, he felt himself naked and alone, facing a force that was anonymous, invisible, and everywhere.

One morning, after Yulia had left, a new thought occurred to him. As a boy, he'd often found pleasure in writing little stories with which he impressed the adults. And he recalled his wife's passing claim to a great literary lineage (she'd once mentioned that she was related to the 19th-century writer Gogol). Here was something he could do on his own. Instead of going out, he sat up in bed with a paper and a pad and wrote a poem. It came easily, so he wrote another, and then another. That evening he read his creations to his wife while she peeled beets for their borscht. At first Yulia was touched – this was a side of her husband she hadn't seen before – and she encouraged him by praising his clumsy verses. Over time, however, Yulia, unimpressed by her famous literary ancestor who, she'd heard, had been an unworldly eccentric, a fop, and quite possibly a pervert, began worrying that her husband's new hobby was distracting him from earnest demands. Life in the free world was expensive. Nowhere more so than Manhattan.

Serge wasn't discouraged. He had outwitted Nazis, Stalinists, and his father. The new city, with its towering buildings a backdrop to the ardor and ambitions of its frenzied folk, proved a goad and a catalyst. The kingdom of God was within, which meant his resources were fathomless – this truth his father had taught him, and to it he cleaved.

Absorbed by his poems, Serge ignored his wife's complaints about their apartment and their prospects. "Ineluctable modality of the visible," he whispered to himself. In poetry he at last found what he'd been looking for. There were constants amid the world's endless transformations. Sestinas and sonnets thrilled him. They proved design amid chaos, in the patterns on a ladybug's wings, the ocean's tides, the magic of fractals. His mind blazed with the truths flowing from his spontaneous pen.

4

The O'Connells were from a banking family. A civic-minded couple, they threw frequent parties for the Hibernian elite. On such evenings, Yulia would be asked to stay late with the twins, at the far end of the hall. Because she would occasionally need to consult with Moira O'Connell, Yulia always wore her best dress, a red ruffled thing which cunningly highlighted her breasts. In her late twenties, the former child actress, with her blond hair and blue eyes, invariably magnetized the attention of the men in the room. Emitting invisible waves of welcome, Yulia beamed in reply. Ever the hostess, Moira O'Connell always took a moment to introduce her nanny to whomever she happened to be speaking, including the recently elected young president, John Kennedy, about whose exploits at the Carlyle Moira O'Connell frequently gossiped with friends. She also met the charming and flamboyant congressman, the six-foot-four Yale graduate, John Lindsay, who would, a few years later, become New York City's mayor before illness and the absence of health insurance eventually left him destitute and depleted. Moira's parties were attended by the likes of journalist Jimmy Breslin, the actress Maureen Stapleton, even Gene Kelly! In the late fifties and early sixties, everyone radiated excitement – they had just won a world war, and nothing could stop them.

Evenings at the O'Connell's made her life with Serge, in their one-bedroom apartment whose bathtub was located squarely in the middle of the kitchen, feel like a sepia nightmare, and though she tried to conceal her dissatisfaction from her husband, she found it harder to hide her restlessness from herself. She stopped telling him stories about the glamorous people she'd met on her job, and never mentioned the nickname given her by some of the men – Zsa Zsa – after the busty, blond Eastern European actress she faintly resembled.

Serge, meanwhile, kept slipping backward. A letter from a cousin informed him his parents had both died during a tuberculosis epidemic that swept through Mexico City. He dreamed his mother stood before him with her arms outstretched, like she was poised to fly, or be crucified. "This is how we displace air," she said soothingly. And Serge was sure he sometimes heard his dead sister calling to him as he walked the streets. How did she find him? he wondered. How did she know his name?

Serge struggled. On the one hand, he'd inherited his father's instinct for justice. Back in Chile, he'd once broken the arm of man who had raised his whip to a dog. Meanwhile, from Yulia he'd heard countless tales of lost grandeur – even if what she repeated were her own mother's stories, which were themselves largely embroideries on fables she'd heard her mother tell about *her* grandmother's life in the time of the Cossacks in the 17th century – and these fantasies gave rise to a sense of stolen entitlement, as though he too had been cheated of a birthright along with his wife. On bad days, when he couldn't find work, or write, or, as happened more and more often, his wife seemed unreachable, he told himself his soul had been insulted in centuries past. He was the son of kings and he and his children after him deserved to wear a crown. He felt his soul's nobility: We are promised a great destiny, even if its ultimate fulfillment flowers only in paradise at the end of time. These internal contradictions fueled his verse. But what do you do with poems no one will publish? Who are you really writing for? What do you hope to achieve? Do you seriously imagine sustaining a family on a suite of sonnets, no matter how numinous?

Eventually, Serge fell to earth. One evening, Yulia arrived home to find him asleep, with an open book by William Blake resting on his face. Tired after caring for the twins, she exploded: "What do you think you're doing?" She unleashed a litany of frustrations he was shocked and startled to hear. "Nobody needs your poems," she shouted, unknotting her babushka, freeing her shimmering mane.

Serge blushed with shame. He had failed, yes, failed miserably. He and his work would be forgotten – as though anyone remembered it now. The waters would close over him and the rest would be silence. How dare he take his wife and future children down with him merely for the sake of his own dreams?

He had once been a practical man, first to rise, first to arrive on the job, first to volunteer for the riskiest tasks, provided there was a bonus for accepting the challenge. He would recover his former ways; he would show Yulia that, even in these new circumstances, he could provide. With good health and such an attitude, how could he fail?

And for a time it looked like his program would work. He

and Yulia reconnected, taking Sunday walks in the park after mass at the Orthodox church on 82nd Street (born Greek Catholic, Yulia moved fluidly among the various Abrahamic sects, depending on the preferences of her husband or lover of the moment), or going to movies on Saturdays. Among their favorite films were *Breakfast at Tiffany's, West Side Story*, and *The Misfits*. Seeing *A Raisin in the Sun*, about a black family's struggles to move ahead in the world, Serge heard the voice of his father, and a dormant political side of him began to stir. Back in Texas, both of them had been shocked by the dirty looks they earned from white people when they sat next to blacks on buses. They had heard about American racism, of course, but they hadn't seen it until they crossed the border. This was another new experience they tried to make sense of, until they realized that it made no sense whatsoever and was an example of a local madness; though Serge said he thought it wasn't all that different from the tribal tensions between neighbors back in the old country, where, not that long ago, human beings had been owned and traded and sold – wasn't that what Yulia's relative Gogol had written about?

After years of moving between short-term jobs, largely in restaurants, Serge found steady work at *The New York Times* printing plant. He lasted over a year, until the day the Typographical Union's president called a strike. On hearing this, Serge sighed – strikes reminded him too much of his father's stories about the old country.

For the first month he used his free time to revise some poems he'd been working on. He also applied himself in practical ways, repairing their vacuum cleaner, fixing leaks, and even rewiring the lights in the apartment. By February, however, things got tougher. Yulia told him she was pregnant.

5

Serge sat alone at the bar in the White Horse Tavern nursing his Pabst. He surveyed the other patrons arrayed along the rail before settling on a young woman with her red hair under a cap. He watched the way her full lips clamped the beer bottle.

For all his devotion to his wife, Serge's vigor was not readily contained by one partner, and along the way Yulia found herself having to share her richly-muscled, bright-eyed young husband. At first, his infidelities left her nonplussed. Like him, she'd survived a war: entire cities had been wiped out around them. Half her family had been murdered by one side or the other. If Serge had a lover or two along the way, well, he was a man and could hardly be expected not to act like one. Even rumors of children dropped here and there didn't shake her.

Despite her husband's lapses, she knew Serge loved her. She could tell from the way he looked at her, how he held her in bed on those nights when she hadn't banished him to the couch. She was in charge.

The one sin – and she believed in sin, in good and evil and the

Devil, and Heaven and Hell, and said nightly prayers to the Virgin Mary, whom she revered above even her favorite Saint Sarvo the bear-lover – the one sin Yulia could not abide was poverty. Her husband's inability to capitalize on his gifts and grow rich was proof of weakness, and worse, of God's disapproval. This she could not accept. And she told him so, brusquely, directly. Pressured by unpaid bills, she shouted, calling her husband a bum, a failure, unable to provide for the family he had pretended to want. What did she need him for if she was the one paying the rent? Forgotten were the early years back in Mexico, when the birds of the air were all the entertainment she needed and the ground beneath their feet all the home she could want. Forgotten were the whistles, gropings, and insults of her new countrymen in Texas – as well as the many kindnesses extended to the young immigrants by good people everywhere.

It was like he'd become invisible. Even his own wife couldn't see him. Serge recalled his father telling him about his conversation with a French philosopher in Paris after the war: "History is the story of slaves trying to free themselves. But nature commands submission." He was nothing more than a slave, he knew that. But, like his father before him, Serge was not resigned.

6

Oliver was born the day President Kennedy was assassinated. Yulia had just emerged from the delivery room when she overheard the nurses whispering tearfully about events in Dallas. She was in a daze. Her face was covered with sweat. Could it be true – the handsome man she'd met at the O'Connell's dinner party! Tears now sprang to her eyes. She was bewildered – the mix of joy and grief in such close proximity, her best response was to close her eyes and sleep.

She later learned the gunman had spent time in her part of the world. She wasn't surprised. The President's death made her think of the long list of murdered czars and, nursing her boy, she wondered what kind of a world he'd be entering.

*

Unable to find steady work, Serge grew desperate. When an acquaintance on the fringes of Second Avenue's émigré community invited Serge to contribute a column to a weekly paper – for a modest sum, of course – Serge agreed without hesitation, even though he knew rumor had it the paper was funded by the Soviets. But he could not feed a family on rumors. This was work – this was writing! He was flattered and excited. He had a lot to say to his new country. The political implications of his association troubled him – but he had received so little support from "the community". And hadn't his father remained a Communist his whole life? He blamed his father for the rootless existence which had given him no confident space to call his own. He'd read somewhere that random thoughts caused pain – but random thoughts were all he'd had these last years: thoughts about money, home, his parents. He thought about how much he'd loved his mother, and what it meant not to have a country. Writing for "POOR" ("Pals of our Rus") gave him a sense of purpose, along with some cash.

For Yulia, the betrayal was the last straw. How dare he collude with the children of men who'd murdered so many of her friends and family! She told him to leave, and never return. To her surprise, he agreed. Aram was two months old. He never saw his father again.

"Little Fascist Panties"

A FEW YEARS back, Russ was in Chicago for a conference. On a whim he decided to call his cousin Larissa to ask if she was free for lunch the next day. They hadn't seen each other since his mother's funeral four years ago. They'd spoken briefly over finger sandwiches in the drafty, barnlike reception hall between the church and the cemetery in Bound Brook. The afternoon had been a blur of fatiguing encounters; he and Larissa had exchanged only a couple of words. His clearest memory of her was from back when she was twelve, daring in a blue dress and running wild in the back yard at a family gathering. The gatherings, which framed so much of his childhood, finally ended when he went off to college. It had been a relief. When their parents' generation got together, the dead held pride of place. Talk turned to memories of feasting on "roof rabbits" (i.e. cats), explosions in the night, lost friends. No wonder the new generation wasn't interested in maintaining ties. They scattered across the country like fugitives afraid to look back. His mother's funeral had been a reunion of shadows.

Larissa and Russ agreed to meet at a fusion sushi bar on the North Side. A mid-March sun sliced the sky that lowered over the whitecaps on Lake Michigan. Water filled the window of the cab. How was this not an ocean, or at least a sea?

After an awkward peck on the cheek, they sat down and immediately dove into the menu. Once the waitress had brought them their drinks (white wine for her, cranberry juice for him), they finally focused on each other.

"So what do you think is up with our family?" he asked. The words tumbled out. Seeing Larissa in this new context broke the lock on a door he'd shut years ago. Who knew what else might emerge?

She'd been a pretty girl and had grown into an attractive woman, except for the obvious tension she seemed to hold between her finely sculpted brows.

"Wow," she laughed. "Good morning to you, too!" She shook her head. "You're the first person in the family to ask such a direct question. I've been wondering about it myself for years." She put her hand to her forehead. He noticed how long and strong her fingers looked. They must have given her an advantage on the cello.

Specifically, Russ wanted to ask about her twin brother, but couldn't bring himself to do it. Her twin brother had recently been found dead, of auto-erotic asphyxiation, which didn't completely surprise Russ, given that business with her father.

The twins' father had been committed to a psychiatric facility after he attemped to shoot his wife on Christmas eve. Apparently the gun misfired. Holidays are hell. Her mother had died soon after, of unrelated causes, and the twins were raised by an aunt in Winnipeg while the father was confined to an asylum.

The war, which had forced their family to flee their native city, had been over for half a century, but it didn't seem completely over yet.

A halogen beam spot-lit Larissa's hair. Her skin looked lit from within. She became serious. "There was a time," she confessed, "when I thought I'd wind up living on the street." Her face grew darker. She wore a tight, brief, black wool skirt with black stockings down which she raked those strong fingers. Her almond-streaked hair was pulled in a thick ponytail. She might have been dressed for the stage. For all Russ knew, she had a performance that evening.

The Japanese waiter glided silently between the counter and the sleek metal tables scattered around the hip, pumpkin-colored, high-ceilinged dining room. A mirror across from the counter – a nod to the old Chicago saloons – doubled the scene.

"You too?" Russ nodded. "In my twenties, I lived at the Y for nearly a year. I worked at a copy place during the day and drank at night."

"I once tried counting all the hairs on my head," Larissa admitted.

"How far did you get?"

"Always lost it when I hit five figures." She flashed five fingers as the fish arrived.

She smiled and he wondered where she got her looks. Her mother had been a dowdy woman with fat legs and large breasts she never tried to conceal. At fifty-three, Russ was eighteen years older than Larissa.

"Wanna blow a joint?" he said out of nowhere.

"You carried pot on the plane?"

"Everybody needs a bit of madness in their lives," he said before remembering who he was talking to.

The waiter brought another glass of wine.

"We can go to my place," she said, swirling the pale liquid before downing it in two gulps. Once in her car, she tightened up again. Her face scrunched. It was a Thursday afternoon and the traffic was heavy but she pressed on, pedal to metal, cutting off a motorcyclist who flashed the finger in protest. The panel on a truck declared: *Free the Bears!* More clouds rolling in from the west tried to smother the sun. She hit the brakes. His thumbs bit his knees. A threat of snow hung in the air.

"This is the winter of my discontent," he said.

"Why's that?"

"I'm over fifty. Divorced. No kids. I have an excellent job but what good does that do anyone – or even me, for that matter?"

"For fifty you look good. Good for forty, for that matter. I'm thirty-five."

"Women are at their best in their mid-thirties," he said.

"Good to know I'm in my prime."

"Takes until your mid-thirties to pull things together," he explained.

She shook her head. "You're full of happy talk, aren't you? We must be related. At least you have a good job. You don't have that to complain about."

"Don't you love your work?" he asked.

They were stopped at a light. Russ wiped the staff of sweat from his upper lip, which still felt funny without the moustache. She'd pulled so near a bus he could see the rust edging the rivets. When she didn't answer, he said:

"You look great."

Immediately he felt embarrassed. What had gotten into him? He'd been right to steer clear of family. Hadn't seen anyone from his clan in years. A silence settled over the car. Larissa turned on the radio but switched it off when the announcer began detailing a car bombing in Baghdad. Finally, after cutting off an old lady in a Civic, Larissa grinned and said:

"Don't worry, we're almost there. I'm really not that drunk."

"It's the others I worry about," he said.

"Fuck 'em," she blasted back. Then she reached over and

lifted the lid on the seat divider where she kept dollar bills, make-up, and candy bars, and pulled out a cigarette.

"Mind?" She tapped her steering wheel in a gesture he hadn't seen since his thirties, when he and all his circle smoked. "I'll join you," he said though he hadn't had one in years.

"How's the cello?" he asked.

"I gave it up," she sighed, nearly sideswiping a girl on a bicycle. Russ watched the pink helmet flash by.

Her news struck him like word of a death.

"You played so beautifully."

"There's beautiful and then there's beautiful," she said.

"Weren't you in an orchestra?"

She clucked her tongue and shook her head.

"Here we are," she said, screeching into the underground garage below a windswept apartment building right on the lake.

During the elevator ride neither spoke. Entering the foyer, which was larger than Russ's entire apartment, she said, "Now I can have a real drink. Another cranberry juice?"

"No thanks. Where's your bathroom?"

After washing his hands he looked over the books stacked on a small stone column: Swafford's *Brahms; Alexander Technique Part I; Wolf Hall.* The rose-colored towels were of thick Egyptian cotton. In the living room he stood before the picture window and watched rush hour congealing below. It was a little after four. Larissa, meanwhile, had taken off her heels and curled up on the chocolate brown couch, upholstered in velvety fabric. Before joining her, he stopped to study a framed document hanging on the wall.

"Whoa! This really De Niro's signature? And his parents?"

She'd been thinking deeply on the whiskey she coddled in both hands.

"Bobby De Niro, age fifteen," he read from the plaque. "His freshman report card. Incredible."

She patted the couch beside her. "Sit here," she said. Her voice was soft as snow.

He thought again of the twelve-year-old girl in the blue dress running through the garden. The terrible thing with her father happened soon after. By then, Russ had been living in Boston for more than a decade.

"May I ask what this is doing here?" He persisted, settling down beside her, so close he could smell her almondy perfume. Her hair had come loose, spraying her shoulders. Her skirt had pulled up, revealing a run in her stocking.

"A boyfriend knew I had a crush on De Niro. He was into autographs and such."

She pouted, closed her eyes, dropped her head to her chest like she was falling asleep. He stared at her profile. She looked nothing like anyone else in the family, which was good. Then, somewhat operatically, like a sail slapped by a sudden gust, she tipped to the left and fell right into Russ's lap.

*

Russ lay across the bed in the dark, alternately watching headlights snake along the lake and Larissa, who appeared to be examining her breasts in the mirror. Smoke from a joint in the ashtray ballooned in the air like a genie. A Tori Amos song sounded from the clock radio.

There had been a war, he reminded himself. Long ago and far away, and yet not. There had been a czar, but he had been shot. And the burning wheatfields, where were they?

An agitated Larissa cursed, struggling to fasten her bra.

"Need a hand?"

"I've got it."

"This is quite a view. How can an administrator, even at a fancy prep school, afford such a place?"

He stretched his bare arms over his head.

"Alimony," she answered, then: "Fuck!" She sank to the edge of the king-sized bed to wrestle with a black stocking.

And yet they come off so easily, Russ mused.

Slightly stoned, she lurched over to the armchair where the rest of her clothes had been tossed.

"You in a rush?" he asked.

"I have a date," she said. "Picking me up here in" – she looked at the clock on the teak dresser – "forty-seven minutes."

"Ah. Anybody I'm related to?" Russ sat up, scratching under his arm.

"You do have a nasty side," she said. "I knew it. It's in the books."

"So you've read them."

She was pinching her cheeks in the near dark. He could see himself shirtless on the bed sitting behind her as she puckered her lips.

She'd just slipped back into the black skirt when there was a knock on the bedroom door. He'd been surprised when she pulled it shut behind them.

The door opened. Light from the hall blinded them both. Startled, Russ found himself staring at a short bald man with a thick gray handlebar moustache and a medicine-ball belly who appeared as surprised as he.

"What's up, Dad?" Larissa sighed, frowning.

"Sorry, sorry," the man blustered. "Didn't ... forgot ... reading glasses." He turned from Larissa to Russ. His hands rose and fell before him like he was trying to hush an anxious child. At the same time, his short, squat fingers wiggled as though testing a piano.

"Hurry up. Dad, this is Russ. You remember Russ? Sheila's son?" Larissa snapped, her face fierce as a falcon's.

"Sorry, sorry," her father repeated. All the same, he didn't retreat. "I'll just ... my glasses ... leave you ..." He coughed into his fat fingers while staring at Russ. Then he waddled in, and Russ smelt a heavy cologne that might have been Old Spice. The old man went straight for the night table, picked up a pair of glasses with red frames that Russ hadn't noticed, and waddled to the door. Before crossing the threshold, he turned and asked, his voice guttural, like his throat was coated with phlegm: "Drink, anyone?"

"Dad!"

"No thank you, sir," Russ managed to whisper.

"Suit yourselves," he shrugged, shutting the door.

In the dark, Russ felt the shades from his early years gathering around him – or maybe it was just a draft from the hall. He remembered hearing only a few vague details about the trial. Nobody wanted to talk about it, and the papers in Boston hadn't offered much. This was before social media began broadcasting every moment worldwide. When Larissa's father, a physics professor and amateur clarinetist, aimed that gun at his wife on Christmas morning, no one in the family was surprised. The only thing that puzzled them was why the gun had failed. At the same time, no one doubted the insanity plea was sincere. Russ had assumed the man would spend the rest of his days in some mid-western equivalent of Bellevue. Apparently he'd been judged ready to re-enter society.

For a minute after he left, the two cousins said nothing. Then Larissa rose from the bed, went to the closet, and took out a pair of dauntingly high black boots. She sat back down on the bed to pull them on. It was nearly six-thirty. Russ was hungry again.

"How long has he been living with you?" he finally asked.

"Two years. He spent a year in a halfway house after his release. It was an awful place. The other men were so creepy. I just couldn't leave him there."

She looked at Russ like she hoped he understood. But as for understanding, he no longer tried. War; booze; genes. Opportunity.

Outlined only by the light of the Chicago night, he listened to their breathing, wind shuddering the glass.

"How is he?"

"He's not himself," she said, turning on a lamp by the mirror. "I don't know. I mean, I hardly remember what he was like. He lives in his own world. He's very sweet to me. He mainly reads books about birds and quarks and listens to Telemann. Sometimes he goes down to the waterfront and feeds the gulls and the pigeons. Comes back worked up and tells me about the birds he's seen."

Russ couldn't think of anything else to ask. He got up and began dressing.

"See my cell phone anywhere?"

She waved her hand: "There, under the bed, by the headboard. No, closer."

"Thanks." He picked it up, flipped it open to make sure the battery hadn't died.

"It's one of those stupid phones," he explained. "I'm amazed it remembers its own number."

"You don't wear underwear?" she asked.

He zipped his pants and finished buttoning his shirt. Dressed, he stood behind her as she pushed in a pear-shaped earring.

"As you now know for certain, and forever."

They finished in silence. She turned away from the mirror. He followed her out of the bedroom into the hall. There was no sign of her father anywhere. It was like Russ had dreamed him. Then he noticed him sitting in the corner in the dark, a silhouette staring out the window at the traffic with his lips slightly parted. He seemed not to register their presence. Larissa went over, put her palm on her father's bald head, then leaned down and kissed it.

Russ looked away. For some reason he felt embarrassed. His eyes locked on Larissa's hips.

"Didn't you have a coat?" Her smile was tighter than ever.

"Just the jacket. Right there," he said, pointing to the couch. He picked it up and went to the door she was holding open for him. Before disappearing from her world forever, he turned once more.

"We never got around to figuring out what's wrong with our family," he shrugged.

Larissa slumped against the door. Her almond hair fell over one eye, and her hands sank to her thighs, which she rubbed nervously. For a moment her face relaxed again. The muscles around her beak went soft.

"Sure we have," she said.

The Criminal Element

1

Choosing to kidnap the priest may be a mistake. I admit it. Nobody cares about Catholics anymore. The church is a franchise, like McDonald's or Burger King. But the move is bound to bring attention to the Institute.

We've considered taking a doctor instead. They're as bad as priests. Worse. They wait till you're sick, till you have no choice. Then they have you and everything you own. Illness is a big part of our death cult. Once, people weren't afraid of dying; they knew it had to happen. Nowadays there's a hope we might escape it completely, so let rip.

My father wanted me to work for the CIA. "Do your country some good," he advised. He hoped in this way to placate the old world ghosts that haunted him periodically. "He's after me again, Mother," I'd complain. "Don't listen," she'd counsel. I'd hide in my room, hunkered down with one of the Great Books of the Western World, until he found me.

"Rake the lawn," he'd insist. Routine preparations for a life of espionage.

You'd never believe how many trees there used to be in New

Jersey. Come fall, you'd think you were in the Black Forest instead of suburbia.

That was long ago. I haven't been back since my parents died.

I never did learn what claim the ghosts had on my temperamental, hard-working father.

It is December, according to man. Christmas approaches. Eventually the Berlin Wall crumbled. East European dissidents became heads of state. Communism was history. Who can say what will happen here in the new millenium?

It won't be just the information superhighway, I assure you. Too many of our presidents have been murderers. Iraqis and Panamanians died in the streets so we could watch Extra in peace.

But what's the date on the real calendar, where God notes: free Poland, unleash Mandela, spill oil on California?

I'm in my study at the Institute, making notes on my Mac. Jose's preparing areppas and squid for lunch. Cooking is his spiritual discipline. The kitchen is his temple. Hot pepper his holy ghost. We are what we do, and daily, each minute, each second, we choose. Soon the five of us meet to discuss the month's agenda. It will be a busy season.

The Institute, where we all lived then, is in a sprawling house in Somerville. It used to be a working-class city, mainly Italian and Irish, streaked with Haitian, Asian, and African. I'd call it cosmopolitan, if that didn't suggest a glamour this place never had. Think of Paris without lights, without art, without original or interesting architecture. Triple deckers, thickets of antennae, rooms decorated with sea shells. Houses like shipwrecks. Islands of lost souls. There are no pockets of flamboyant wealth in Somerville, no Brattle Streets, Rues Vaugirard, Fifth Avenues, or Via Venetos. In the forties, it was the third most densely populated city in the world. After Hong Kong, and I forget where else. Each shanty is flanked on either side by a gas station or a muffler repair shop. Everywhere garages, car wash palaces, auto parts emporia. The working class never shifted allegiance from engine to microchip. Mild-looking Madonnas in ceruleans gowns grace the yards of the older residents. Christmas lights tacked to the shingles, on night and day, make the city seem a poor man's Candyland.

Don't get me wrong, I love it, and how.

The natives toil in these garages, in local factories, stuffing pillows, stocking food on grocery shelves, selling papers, serving, tending bar, typing letters for insurance agents or third-rate lawyers, plowing roads for the DPW, minding tills in hardware stores, scraping pasta dishes in restaurant kitchens; they're the regular people of this world. Passably thrifty (but we are a debtor nation), industrious (though leaving time in the day for seven hours of television), and undeniably good. Through the window I see a woman tossing bits of hotdog bun to the birds; rumpled Barney in his mashed fedora rapping with the brats returning from school. Little acts of kindness abound. When Anthony's Bar caught fire, Willie, who owns the pizza joint across the street, raced into the burning box to save Emilio's black Japanese goldfish.

These people even seem to like what they do.

For that, I hate them. They let themselves be the coal and the oil in the stoves and the roaring furnaces of the rich.

I'd rather they were the dynamite.

I think a lot about our former president. He and I are linked. We're tied, kin, in cahoots. I know it. How else explain why he outraged me so? I took his decisions personally. I felt responsible. He was my man in Washington. He was an extension of my will, my belief, my desires. Am I wrong? "You take life too personally," my ex-wife said, with never a hint of what else I might focus on.

If the president vetoed a bill I supported, or appointed a judge whose disinterest I doubted, I grieved. I wanted to call, explain his mistake to him. When he cut certain programs, I brooded: was I really that mean, that selfish?

It wasn't just the president that worried me. It was his wife, his marriage, his dog. Were they happy? Did they not see that our interests were twined, and competition a ruse?

2

Wasyl's in the next room, studying the *Bhagavad Gita*. He dropped acid this morning – hence the music, the spasmodic laughter.

He's of the Slavic persuasion. It's bad for him to read religious books. He's shaky, nervous. Thinks he's a poet. Recites Whitman at me. "Song of Myself", Democratic Vistas, "The Sleepers". Good memory. And to him it's news. He contains multitudes. He's eager (far too eager, I want to tell him, but will teach him instead) to sound his barbaric yawp on television. He's also tall, nice looking, and charming when not high. I recognize the temperament. Doomed, utterly doomed. Of course, at his age (twenty), doom's the thing. He's delighted to be doomed. He can't wait to die, flamboyantly, and in public. Preferably on prime time.

It won't be easy weaning him off these religious texts. I know the pull. He responds without knowing to what. Nor has he any sense of how to reconcile youth's frenzies with the discipline of a true religious calling. We'll have to have it out before long.

It'll be harder curing him of MTV.

The young naturally incline toward slime and the sublime, romantic love and narcissistic lust. I speak from experience. They can't bear the clarity of plain adult corruption. Too crude for hypocrisy, they settle for the franker lies at the extremes. They're Gnostics. Manichaeans. I aim to help them integrate.

Besides, he's hot for Deirdre. And I've seen the way she bends in his direction, as though reminding him of her breasts, how she drops her flecked blue eyes when he stares, or how her anxious hand flies to her hair, fingers flitting between loose strawberry clumps like fat, flustered birds.

Do either of them know I know? I don't think so. Therefore, I can play.

Are squirrels willing to die for their trees? To armor themselves in suits of leaf and twig and hurl chestnuts at each other? I mean, I get the business of guarding the nest. That I understand. It's the question of the tree that interests me. Its roots go underground. They're nibbled by grubs, they overlap with other trees. Impossible to say just where they end.

On roots: people won't say much about just what their daddies did for them. How they set them up in the world. Did the president? Not often, not much. Yet was he more than his daddy's shadow?

3

Deirdre watches another invasion on television. She wears a lace nightie I gave her last Christmas: whorls of transparent beige over her breasts. On the screen, soldiers in dappled green and brown race through a maze of shacks hugging rifles close to their chests. Cut to a scene downtown: people exit stores clutching consumer goods, including radios, computer games, clothes. Cut to a scene of the president hunting quail. They don't look hard to kill. Back to the invasion: houses burning, bodies in the street. The stubby fingers of her left hand pinch a nipple. Her other hand moves too. It's not clear who is slaughtering whom and for what. A herd of neatly dressed men and women stand on a hill, raising cans of cola to the sky. She takes the empty rum flask and presses its mouth to her lips. A journalist blabs earnestly about the big push, the high spirits of the poor, many of whose shacks are burning. Peasants cheer the soldiers. Finger in mouth like a Popsicle, the other hand restless.

The revolution: the words heft her to a hill on which she sees herself standing in silhouette, fist accusing the sky. Or she sees herself kicking a nun – Sister Mary Ann, maybe – in the stomach, with a steel-toed shoe, pressing that boot down on the withered lips she'd seen so often mouthing the rosary or scolding her students, breaking down in the middle of a lesson on the Pythagorean theorem, screaming about how the Devil wanted their souls and how he'd get at them through their bodies, her white face twisted, like braided dough with a punched hole for a mouth, and her words bursting out like pebbles of fire. She'd once slapped Deirdre three times when she caught her in a lie, then made her sit on her hands at the head of the room while she lectured, and Deirdre's soul shrank to a thistle of wrath.

Deirdre will never have children. She has no wish to make more people.

There are terrible vibes around me, coming from my fellows at the Institute. I feel them acutely.

Humans are very tough on each other. But they need to learn somehow.

Because real-life lessons occur outside the university, a place such as the Institute for Imaginative Living is indispensable. We study the things they don't teach you in school. Our students bone up on betrayal, blackmail, beating, chicanery, corruption, cruelty, embezzlement, fanaticism, flattery, flirtation, fraud, incest (via role play), lying, racism, sexism, stealing from petty cash, etc. – all in a structured environment. We teach ambition, greed, lust, jealousy, rage. We drive people into these states so they can later learn to control them. It's not easy. But, as I said to Wasyl: no pain, no gain.

There are reasons we Americans need such an education, now as never before in our history. There's no draft around to teach our boys the ways of men. Only a select few, an elite, see first hand what people are capable of. This leaves us vulnerable. Those whose parents suffered under brutish third world regimes enjoy an advantage. Followed by kids whose fathers trained in Iraq, Vietnam, Korea, or WWII. Unfortunately, as we know, young people discount their parents' truths.

Of course, we have no students. There are just the five of us for now. But the core is strong, the center holds. And will, until the time comes to explode.

There is no effect without a cause. The lightning that breaks in singing branches over Winter Hill this morning is but the discharge of static electricity from the massed clouds swarming over us on this December day. The bird feeder on the ground was knocked from the window by a squirrel disappointed by the scraps Deirdre tossed it. The reason Comrade Kesselburger retches in the john is because of last night's round of Jim Beam – probably in company with one of his lady friends from that bar in Boston's lost Combat Zone. I'm not worried. Comrade K will pull through. After puking, he'll shamble back into his study and write verses for two hours. (I don't think I've ever met an American who hadn't at one time or another been a writer.) By lunch, when we have our meeting, he'll be fully restored.

Jose puts the plate of squid down in the middle of the table. I spear a rubbery tentacle. Sushi-style.

I stare at the marbled rose elbow, the pale suction cups.

Wasyl sticks to the areppas, toasted, with cheese.

There's little talk during the meal. K hiccups. Jose hums.

"Oil bill's outrageous."

"Don't pay."

"Ah, that's the one thing you can't do, even as a revolutionary —"

"Gotta pay your bills," Deirdre smiles, easing his dismay. "In fact, kid, where's your share? Haven't you been handing out those coupons in the Square?"

"We need paper, or there won't be any more newsletters."

"Charge for it, charge for it, then you won't have to worry."

"You mean, force the people to pay for the truth? No way. Then we'd be no different from them."

"Your turn with the dishes," Jose adds to his burden. And if that's not enough:
"And when the liberating's done? What will we do?"

"Money. We'll make money."

We chose the priest from St Michael's because he should have known better. Deirdre and I have listened to his sermons. We attended some dozen masses before concluding he was our man. It wasn't even boring. I remembered going to church with my parents. Father staring gravely at the golden candlesticks. Mother looking pious, mouthing prayers.

Wasyl's trying to understand this desperate place in which he finds himself. He cranks the volume up on the TV. How crucial television is, even with the web, to literary types of the next generation. The least taste of it nurtures a craving.

"It's the world," Wasyl explained. "The Big Picture. You see everything. It's global, man. How else can you get perspective?"

You know what's missing from the scene today? Character. No one has character anymore. People treat people like they were television. Tired of this conversation? Sick of that peculiarity? Weary of her accent, the same small breasts, the semi-hard penis? Turn the channel. Pop in a movie. Go to a bar. Dial for sex. Shazam! Another world rises. The new begins.

No effect without a cause. But who can isolate that cause inside a sentence?

My cousin never claimed he had a soul left. He knew he'd struck a Faustian bargain. That's not so with priests and popes.

4

I walk up Highland Avenue, past the variety store, recently bought by a Pakistani couple, who hired a local kid to front for them after someone broke their window, and around the corner from Anthony's, past the shop selling baseball cards, the Laundromat, the antique store next to the rock-climbing center (you read about them in the paper only when they fall).

I'm a stranger here, staring blankly in the windows, puzzled by the zeal with which people engage in these deadening tasks. What drives them, I wonder. What do they hope to achieve? For whom are they working?

Racing clouds skim the city. There's no breaking through anymore. Just keep moving, place to place, doing laundry, collecting baseball cards.

And today everyone's Irish. It's one of those days. A glance tells the story. Blue eyes blinking everywhere. Some days it's Jews, others Italians, or blacks. Rarely Turks or Armenians. I check to make sure I'm wearing no orange. No green, either. Because they'll find out. This cosmopolitanism's a veneer. They'll see I'm not one of them. And they'll hunt me down. And they'll string me up. Then smoke me and serve me with kippers. Are kippers Irish or English? Excuse me – British. What, for that matter, are kippers? How are you feeling today? Oh, quite kipper, thank you. Care for a kipper, kiddo? Kip kip, and all that sort of rot. So much to remember. Such signals to learn. How not panic?

The high school on my left is a fine building, on the outside. Clean, fortress-like. Inside, the kids carry guns, shoot each other, steal, rape, soon AIDS, worse than heart attacks because it's death by sex. By love. Which shouldn't happen.

Two kids wielding hockey sticks and wearing baseball caps run by. Suddenly I feel the urge to join them, start running myself, follow them toward their field of play.

Instead, I keep walking. Heavy, old, lost.

Everything is possible, nothing necessary.

My ex-wife said I practice a politics of bitterness. Bitterness? Ah, no, I'd reply: betterness. I reject *what is* because I believe things can always be better.

And does the philosophy work? If one can speak of a philosophy working. To tell the truth, I'm losing faith. How close we come to achieving what we want. How close. And how surprising the obstacles that arise, over and over, making perfection seem possible, and just out of reach. Don't kid yourselves: I want to be healthy. I want to want the same things you want. The mother pushing the stroller: she's done it. How?

Lately my life's shining through the fray of theory, and it frightens me. I duck into Patty's Lunch for coffee. A group of boys crowds round the video in the doorway. They part politely, letting me pass. Waiting for my coffee, I study them, these beings infected by health, possibility, the future. They're wearing Catholic school uniforms. Probably from St Michael's. The priest's face, draped with flesh, pissed me off. His blue eyes: cliché, cliché. Those ridiculous robes. The whole costume in this age of geopolitics, ICBMs, IUDs. A smug shaman in a post-Jetson's world.

Through the window I study the Greek blue of the sky, clouds gone, the trees dark charcoal stubble, and everywhere plumes of spirit, visible evidence of our miserable human souls flowering also from the lips and nostrils of the passersby, hurrying to their offices and shops. People have something strange inside their heads, a peculiar lodestone dragging them this way and that. It's fear that drives them, fear of the street, of the poorhouse, that beats the drum to which they step. This society keeps people scared. That's how it works. It scares them with threats: of the street, foreclosure, Chapter 11. Such shadowy glimpses of the future keep people in line, keep them imprisoned. Keep the heart tight. Money rules. Look over your shoulder: Money rules. Don't trust anyone: money rules. Mother and father? Don't kid yourself, money rules there too. Family life floats on the tide of currency. Does your family love you? Maybe. But can they show their love by helping you? Not if they're poor. What is it like, being poor? I'll tell you. It means heart beating fast night and day; means not looking into your neighbor's eyes; means steady pressure around the heart, sweating, dry mouthed; means not going into stores because you're scared the clerk will wave your bad check around; means not answering the phone and then losing it anyway; means shame; means rage at everyone, not just the people in nice cars, but them especially. You're tired of saying to yourself: well, in third-world countries, millions have no heat, millions are hungry, are homeless. But you live *here*. Rage, night and day. Often stifled, often submerged, often transformed. But *there*, pulsing below. The poor divorce at twice the rate of couples with money. The poor live in dangerous neighborhoods in high-risk families. Everyone knows how vulnerable the poor are. Even the weather knows. The weather persecutes the poor. Trailer parks in Kansas get wiped out in a twinkling and towns in Florida are destroyed overnight.

As to the ex-president, I have a confession to make. He's not my cousin. He is no relation to me. None. And what do I know of the pope? Nothing. Not even his name.

There's Deirdre, driving by. My God. Those lips. It's not right for an anarchist to so love the flesh; yet I do. I love a woman's hair, and shoulders, and smell. I'd like to swim ten thousand seasons in the sea of one woman, without shore.

Wasyl's with her. He's talking. Always talking.

What worries me – there's always something – is the car, a Yugo '82, a nice machine, dented and tired, which sometimes goes quiet as a cat in the middle of traffic. What if we have a priest and are racing away and the car dies?

Sometimes I enjoyed mass. I felt a twinge once or twice. Near the end, when people turn to each other and shake hands. How curious and, in a way, beautiful the whole business was. The colored lights in the painted glass, the costumes, the candles. And then strangers suddenly turning to each other. Flickers of compassion, connection.

I hate the church because it's so near the truth it's intolerable. The cross is like the atom diagrammed, confusing people until they find a way of seeing through it, seeing beyond. Who wouldn't love it, when you stop to think? Who wouldn't weep?

Maybe we should just forget the priest.

The girl behind the counter. Greasy white outfit, blue striped collar. I see through it, to the figure underneath, its glorious promise and hunger.

After my wife left – suddenly, no warning, though she claimed there were signs aplenty – I began reading the Bible, looking for what it said about love between men and women. And you know what? Nothing. Nothing there. Every reference to love has to do with God. Any wonder things screw up in this arena? The Bible never specifically prohibits screwing in sand dunes or saunas, with teachers and their girlfriends, or exotic dancers using devices ... nothing is said. We're permitted to merge with all the ghosts of the flesh willing to play. It doesn't teach you how to tell love from lust.

Maybe I should have listened to the old man. Joined the CIA. Hitched to Alaska. Gone whaling.

I look around. The place is empty. The girl cuts cheese on the slicer, her back to me. Done, I push away from the counter and head for the door. The cold welcomes me back.

A Brief History of the Little : People

A national security letter is an administrative subpoena issued by the United States federal government to gather information for national security purposes. NSLs typically contain a nondisclosure requirement, frequently called a "gag order", preventing the recipient of an NSL from disclosing that the FBI had requested the information.

Wikipedia

OUTSIDE, THE SUN is shining. It is June 9, 2019. The president has just returned from England where he dined with the Queen, insulted the mayor of London, and tweeted his support for a whack-job with a plummy accent running for Prime Minister. Meanwhile, for the record, concentration camps have been set up along the Texas/Mexico border.

Nevertheless, coffee gets drunk. I walk the four blocks to Mystic Roasters where I'm stuck behind a young woman who has ordered a mocha soy latte, which makes me want to scream. I do not want my coffee curated; I do not want a heart scribbled in cream crowning a cup of it. In this, as in other matters, I am in the minority. When my turn finally comes, I've aged a year. Blood sugar's fallen precipitously.

My voice, as I order my pound of Sumatra, ground for espresso, is weak.

*

There are so many things I want to tell you but can't. The letter about which I can't speak: I can't get it out of my mind. How can people send you a letter saying the one thing you can't do is speak about the letter? I think they're trying to drive me mad. I think it may be working.

*

How you? Joan texts as I hand the young woman my debit card.

Shitty, I reply.

It'll get better. ☺

I swear, if she uses one more emoji ... I know she's trying to help. Many people are. My friends can tell something is up but nobody seems to know what to do, mainly because I can't tell them what's wrong without also getting them in trouble. And this has been going on for two years.

Drink at Harvest? 5?

Brilliant, I reply.

א she texts. I've no idea what she means. I hurry back to my apartment to feed the Little : People.

*

On examining my options, and after considering everything – absolutely everything – I've decided I have no choice but to end it. Who led me astray? Who pulled me from the righteous path? Who persuaded me it was right to pursue whatever dalliances offered themselves? This ends here. It's complicated because I'm a little in love with Grisha. Grisha! So diminutive yet so shapely, collectible as a Hummel, delectable as a dollop of cream. I could fall into her and die happy – except, of course, I'd crush her.

*

My name is Andy Divino, and here's a bit of data: I'm 5'11" and weigh 179lbs. Some muscle. Some fat. Shoe size: 11. Footwear of choice: black Reeboks, though I'm tempted by Allbirds. Everybody (and by everybody, I mean Steven Pinker) says Data is key. Do you know me now? No? More? Hair: dirty blonde, full, thick, on the longish side, parted in the middle. Lips plump. Chin strong enough. Eyes: hazel. I have no tattoos, no obvious marks – unless you yank my pants down to see the hernia scar. Does that do it for you?

What if I add that I live in a small town north of Boston, through which Paul Revere once rode? You know he never shouted the British were coming? Dude never even got to Concord where was fired that shot heard round the world. Brits busted him well shy of there. It was Longfellow pitched the legend. Poets care nothing for data. But Revere did gallop through our town. Did he stay silent because he didn't care what happened here? Some things we'll never know.

And that's not all: Emerson preached in the Unitarian church down the block. History's our leading product, now manufacturing's gone Chinese. We peddle the past like it mattered. The way things are going, we won't have much of future, so we sell what we got.

What if I add that I'm a translator? That I can't tell you who I work for? Sorry, make that past tense: *worked* for.

These days I collect disability and keep to myself. Except for Joan.

*

Home. I drape my jacket on a chair and hurry to the kitchen. Today the lead story on the radio is about a billionaire pedophile, arrested when he stepped off his private jet after a jaunt to Paris: Dom Perignon, Michelin stars, Pigalle. And, man, the dude's *connected*: presidents, nerdy Harvard profs, pudgy royals: people who have everything, except innocence. Which can be bought, it seems. Wonder how this ends.

I turn off the radio and turn to feed my charges.

They're what I've sacrificed everything for. The Little : People have been my secret these last two years. They saved me, after all. They saw how lost I was, how desperately I needed someone who understood me. That they recognized my quest for meaning is beyond incredible. My gratitude will last a lifetime. And yet ...

That's part of what makes everything so tough. There's no explaining this. Not to anyone. This page alone will know why I did what I did, and why today I live as I do.

I pour two fingers of granola into a tiny trough and rush to the living room. They're in the terrarium, pressed against the glass, peering up at me. "Morning," I say. Grisha waves. I set the trough beside her and watch the others rush it. "Thank you," Adam shouts. "My pleasure," I reply.

If you got to know The Little : People, you'd love them too. You'd want to do things for them. Everything. You'd want to do everything for them. Soon you'd want to be them.

The Little : People just want to have fun. Took me a while

to get this. I used to think they were trying to entertain me, make me laugh. Turns out they were simply keeping *themselves* amused. It was their nature they expressed: a love of poetry, frivolity, art, romance, and song. They must be the most fun family on the planet.

All six can say the most outrageous things to each other, yet they never take offense. Yesterday, Adam told his dad he'd sooner die than grow old like him. The old man roared with laughter!

The young man, Adam, fancies himself a bit of a writer. He's working on his second novel. It's the story of Adam and Grisha (which happens to be his sister's name). In the novel, he and Grisha are portrayed as full-size, normal refugees from some unnamed island whose parents are arrested for being in this country illegally, leaving the kids to fend for themselves. Persecuted by an incredibly creepy character whose name I forget at the moment, they're trafficked to a man who uses slaves to peddle fentanyl ... oh it's a tangled tale, which tells you something about the kind of imagination those Little : People have.

Their humor and their imagination: it's why I'm so attentive. Had I not cared for them, who would have? No one, that's who. They'd have died of inanition. It horrifies me to imagine it: these six lovely, delicate, fragile, tiny beings who, until recently, lived in a shoe box! Without me, how would they survive? And yet, I know that if things got desperate, they'd only laugh and hoist a glass. Their high spirits never flag. It's like they have helium for blood, their hearts the open sky.

How had they managed before I came along? You might well ask. I have no answer. I'll say no more about it except that faith itself is stranger and even more mysterious than the Little : People.

What I can tell you with absolute certainty is this: one morning, as I was rummaging through my closet, looking for something other than a pair of sneakers, I picked up an old shoebox. As soon as I touched it, I thought I heard a scream. I paused, holding it away from myself.

No, I said to myself, no. A neighbor. The vents. Sound travels in apartments cheap as mine. And, generally, I don't object to the reminder that I am not alone in the world. Living alone, as I do, or did, or thought I did, either you plunge into social life, haunt bars, concerts, restaurants, the theater, consume culture with all the appetite of the thwarted, or you sink deeper into yourself, into your solitude, your memories and dreams. When you spend too much time alone, the latter often mix in your mind until you can no longer tell the difference: dream or memory?

But these were neither. As I raised the box higher, I again heard voices. Who knows why I didn't freak or how I managed to set the box down calmly on my bed and lift the lid?

*

Today the President insulted every person of color ever to walk the earth. This raised a fuss on social media; the sweethearts at NPR went bananas, of course; but nothing really happened. Nothing changed. Soon everyone was back to binge-watching *The Americans*. NPR leaked hints about the forthcoming *Downton Abbey* flick. Much excitement in the 'burbs.

Joan texts again to remind me about our drink date. Can't wait, I text back before returning to trim the dozen bonsai I've collected to create a forest. Soon the Little : People will have dark woods to explore. Or maybe not.

*

Lately my reading focuses on finding a cure for whatever malignancy besets me. This morning I discovered a relevant passage in a book called Under the Covers: *PTSD in the 21st Century*:

"There a many reasons people keep secrets. For those who habitually suppress information for professional reasons, life may eventually become a series of metaphors. They find themselves unable to say what they mean, either because they would be breaking a confidentiality agreement or because they might have to reveal compromising information about a family member. In repressing their feelings they rechannel them into other interests and obsessions. They begin to live at the level of metaphor. As a result, other metaphors, particularly those associated with various religious and spiritual practices, feel real to them. More real than experience itself. This has consequences."

*

Three generations of the Little : People live with me. At first I didn't understand about the ":". I asked for clarification. You mean you have small gastrointestinal systems? No-no, Adam explained patiently – clearly he'd covered this ground before – it's like the punctuation mark. Colon, kin to semi-colon.

Although philosophers have theorized its history, calling it, invidiously, "the green light of punctuation", I knew, of course, the colon's reputation as the local skank.

My only regret is that I'm not a scientist with a grant from a foundation. I'm perfectly positioned. Since transferring them from the box to the terrarium, I have glimpsed lives which are, for many reasons, extraordinary. There are theological truths I've understood from watching them. To give you one example: they're a very religious bunch. Apparently their faith was repressed in their native land, wherever that may be. It's a subject they don't like to talk about, and I don't want to insist. What they believe in seems a little obscure as well. All I know is, it involves lint.

Joke. Just a joke.

Yes, what's most singular and touching about the Little : People is their unquestioning faith. They believe in God the way most of us expect the sun to rise tomorrow, and the next, *in saecula saeculorum*. Though, of course, the sun doesn't exactly rise, does it? Never mind. God is not in *those* kinds of details.

There's something furious about their faith, something that suggests it's been tested by fire, something that makes me believe in their belief. Yes, it's their theology that interests me above all. Because if I believe in them, and they believe in a higher order, then, thanks to the distributive property, I too believe. I am a believer. Their presence multiplies me and my faith.

Since moving them to the terrarium, I've overheard unforgettable conversations. The generational drama's poignant. When the old ones kvetch about their gut, arthritis, or a gout, the youngest chuckle, saying: *That's because you're getting ready to die, you old fools. Don't you see it?*

The old man has always been a bully – I've heard enough to figure that out. He's from that generation of men some idiot called "the greatest", even though, or maybe because, they participated in history's greatest bloodbath. He pushes everyone around and flares up over nothing. But I've also heard him speaking to his wife in bed at night, confessing that he regrets his temper, adding that he can't help himself. He's like an old dog who's been kicked all his life. The endless generation, I call them.

The Little : People never hide from anything. They never mask their disgust with the world. For people who seem to have spent most, if not all, of their existence in a box in my closet, they're familiar with the grim deeds of our species: our wars, our crimes, our cruelties. Yet their contempt never overshadows their sterling capacity to delight in ordinary things, like the way the shadows from the blinds crawl across the muddy floor of their terrarium (I accidentally spilled part of my coffee into their world the other morning while watching them).

Another worry is what to do when one gets sick. What doctor would know how to treat the Little : People?

Don't worry, Adam assures me, we never get sick. We're built to last. We're durable as rock. Did you know granite was 90% aluminum?

I smile at the uncanny creature with the soft skin and warm brown eyes. They are also a fatally attractive family. This has its dangerous side.

*

Where r u?
On my way!

*

We're sitting at the Harvest bar: wood's so glossy I slick down a cowlick reflected in the counter. I'm sipping an Appletini. Joan peers longingly into her Pinot Grigio – like she wishes she could dive in and stay. I know how she feels.

Then she engulfs the glass with her big, cellist's hand. Years ago, we lived together. Four years. Never married. It's why we're still friends.

I'm tempted to tell her about the letter *and* the Little : People – but I think better of it. She knows I'm in some legal doo-doo I can't talk about. Her gray eyes offer solace. Done deriding politicians who have pushed our world to the brink – the very edge of the path to extinction, a million species doomed – I ask about her family, starting with her sister.

"In remission."

I go down the list. At one time I was close to these people. When Joan broke up with me, so did they. I hadn't realized how much I'd counted on them: her father, John Chantilly, was in the coffee business. A preppie, he was polished, he was fun. Lunch was stories about business with ex-Nazis coffee growers. Now, of course, he sources Fair Trade only – though he says behind the scenes the land's still owned by families whose inner sancta sport the *hakenkreuz.*

"And your mother?"

Helen was a card. Her schtick was making like she could have been a famous actress if her husband hadn't stolen her away from Hollywood where she was raised by Christian Scientists. Helen has studied with shamans from Brazil to Mongolia and reads auras. Sometimes she'd leap up in the middle of a meal to light a torch of sage and pass it over me in a spiritual cleanse.

"Just landed a bit part in a revival of *Hair* on the North Shore."

"Singing?"

"No, but she'll be naked."

A naked seventy-year-old grandmother (Joan's brother has three boys) on stage miles from where Judges

Hathorne, Sewell, Sergeant, Saltonstall, and Stoughton doomed Bridget Bishop to be hanged for witchery. All Harvard men, naturally. Count on the best and brightest to do real harm.

Eventually Joan turns the tables.

"How are you spending your time, Sven?"

As I can't talk about work, or the Little : People, I make up a project, an imaginary translation of an Estonian classic about a man who discovers a colony of tiny beings dwelling in the basement of his house. It is a great and allegorical work, I say – charming, unsettling, and unpredictable.

"That's just what you need," she says, "a big project like that. Tell me about the author."

Which I do, at great length. In this way a civilized evening is passed. Soon it's time to feed my charges again.

*

If the Devil had a lover, he'd sift the tide for starfish cast up from a farther shore and spear them on a grouper's spine to craft a crown he'd fringe with flame before restoring the tiara to its proper place atop the dark brown mane he longed to handle like a whip while hissing in a whorl: *My queen, my whore. My silly, silly queen.* Believe me, I know. I had the Devil for a lover once, and I admit it was "fun" – until it nearly killed me. Her name was Joan. You'd never know it now we're friends, which is all we should ever have been.

*

Reading Adam, I find echoes of my own life. Who among us isn't from some "elsewhere"? Every family's an "elsewhere-verse", with its own laws, values, and hierarchies of power – in the form of money, physical intimidation, absence of conscience. And yet from the strictest clans the fiercest rebels spring.

*

Fuck the letter!

I was recruited. I offered a way in. This will come as no surprise to you. Given my grandfather, I was seen as the perfect candidate for this line of work. Secret work. For a place so deep down it doesn't even have an acronym.

It was my skills as a linguist they coveted. No one else had ever made much of my gifts, and I was flattered.

Ten years I gave them. Until I began waking in night sweats. I dreamed I saw them, the faces of the people I'd hurt – they were smiling at me from another shore, from some place better than our raw deal here. And that's what I told them. You should thank me, I hissed. Look at you, all light-arrayed, and me here getting heavy and glum, having to keep on.

*

I acknowledge it's possible that my work and my solitude have taken their toll. Things aren't making sense in the way they once used to. I wake up sometimes wondering who I am and why I'm still here. I've been told it's not unusual in my line of work. This doesn't cheer me as much as you might think.

*

The Little : People have frequent discussions about sex, which sometimes turn into shouting matches between the sexes, who see things differently. In their culture it's commonplace to put everything on the table. Of course, how much do I really know about their culture? Like, zilch.

Leonard, the father, said to Adam: "There are things you must understand, son. The prettier the girl, the crazier. Women are at their finest in their mid-thirties. After fifty, every woman is a lesbian."

At which point the wife, daughter, and grandma all began shrieking.

"Early onset menopause," noted Leonard dryly. "Ignore them. I have a friend. His wife made him send his penis to re-education camp. She didn't want it acting like a dick anymore. On its return, his penis announced it no longer wanted to be a penis. It wanted to be a baseball glove instead. That way it could count on seeing some action. Everybody loves baseball gloves, especially when they're broken in, the leather worn smooth, blackened, showing suede. You watch out, son. Life's a slippery slope."

The women of the tribe huddled in the corner, whispering among themselves.

*

At work I began hearing rumors my sex life was being examined for impurities. Of which, apparently, there were a few. Quite a few, depending on who was doing the examining. This, of course, was after I filed my complaint – though I was assured the two matters were not related. My complaint, they insisted, had nothing to do with the subsequent investigation into me. I'd never considered any part of my sexual being impure, but the bosses saw things differently. When the first whispers that I was being investigated reached me, I wasn't worried. I had my mother to thank. At least about some things she'd given me the confidence of a king.

My sexually compulsive youth was not a strike against me, my mother assured me, so long as it wasn't over yet. She said it with a poker face during a rare visit. It must have been Christmas. A strange bird, my mother. I wasn't sure how to read her, so I said: "No worries there, lust undiminished."

"Phew," she whistled. "For a minute I was afraid you were buying the bullshit."

"What bullshit is that?"

"All this talk about men and women, and how we hate sex. I have girlfriends in their eighties who still get it on. With men, or without. There are ways, you know."

"So I've heard," I said. Nothing is as simple and as black and white as we're inclined to make it. People need privacy and they need secrets. To grow, the soul needs the dark as well as the light. If the sun were out 24/7, the earth would be a desert and there would be no life on the planet. "In hell," wrote Nietszche, who knew whereof he sprach, "the lights are always on." One popular form of torture, as you know, is keeping someone in solitary with the lights on.

*

Today, a white man wielding an AK-47 shot and killed more than twenty people in El Paso. Was he aware that he wasn't playing a video game? Or was he living at the level of metaphor?

Everyone knows what's wrong with the picture – and so what? Nothing changes. Nothing will change.

*

The state of poetry is a state of justice generated by a state of grace. Nevertheless, the leaky toilet needs to be repaired. The bathroom floor has flooded. While waiting for the plumber, I decided to have a cuppa Irish coffee and listen in to the conversation of the Little : People.

It so happens they were engaged in one of their famous inter-generational theological debates. I was shocked to discover the many angry things they had to say about the Protestant religion, against which they hold a grudge because Martin Luther labeled peasants Satan's spawn. Wealthy princes, with Luther's backing, seized the properties of the church and were happy to have them. Subsequently they judged property sacred.

They never cease to astonish, these Little : People.

To add to the drama, Grisha has decided to convert to Islam. "Our father doesn't disrespect you enough?" Adam asked sharply. "Respect this," Grisha replied, flashing the finger, lips curled in a fishy grimace. "Children, children," cried Thelma, the mom, over the snoring of the grandparents, who'd fallen asleep under the little gazebo I built for them from old Poland Springs bottles.

*

Apropos:

The Little : People are obsessed with Gogol. I have no idea why. Funny thing is, I couldn't read his fiction until I tried translating it. Until then, his words repelled me. Could it be because our families were neighbors once, centuries ago? Did he avoid me because his name continues to echo around the world, finding admirers in exotic lands where people pass their lives outdoors or working in rice paddies or picking lettuce, tobacco leaves, and copper pipes?

*

Half a million Rohingya have been ethnically cleansed from Myanmar by Buddhists led by a woman with a Nobel Peace Prize. Millions from Syria and Iraq are homeless. A million and a half people in Ukraine have been "displaced" – meaning they now have nowhere to live. Moreover, the rainforest is burning, glaciers are melting, and Greenland isn't for sale. The problems are starting to mount.

*

To recap:

Adam, who sees himself as the scribe of the Little : People, is telling future generations their origin myth. I have a mind to dig deeper, maybe beating out Adam by writing the first complete history of the Little : People, as I try to salvage something, anything, from these last several years.

The grandfather seems especially well-informed. Occasionally I pluck him out of the terrarium and bring him into the kitchen where, with the help of a thimble of Glenlivet, his tongue loosens, and he spills.

He tells me that the Little : People were once a warlike tribe perpetually embattled, laying siege or being besieged for centuries before a kind of exhaustion that resembled peace settled over them. They were ultimately roused from their torpor when a great Teacher came along. The Teacher was no airy-fairy preacher or snake-oil salesman. No, he was a true scholar who pored over profit-and-loss statements and based his prophecies on economic sine curves and trends. He traced the evolution of private property to the abolition of serfdom and the subsequent rise of the state to the accumulation of capital caused by the production of excess product in monasteries wanting income and needing to protect it. Eventually, he said, the entire country was corrupted by what he called the money sickness. Every aspect of life was fiscalized. Air itself became a luxury.

*

This morning they found the billionaire pedophile hanging in his cell. How this happened no one knows. No tears are shed. Many gloat. Others complain he escaped justice. Personally, I'm sure it's murder, and everyone's implicated, from the American president and that toadying Attorney General to a British Royal – not to mention a coven of Harvard geniuses. Mercy, what's become of us?

*

Adam and I often discuss art and literature. He is full of theories. His actual experience of the world has been circumscribed. Yet, though he's lived most of his life in a shoebox, he's somehow managed to project himself far beyond his senses. He must be clairvoyant, or a poet – he looks at us and discovers dimensions in the great world beyond his terrarium, and he dreams, and what he dreams inevitably comes to pass. I approach his every page with trepidation and, of course, a magnifying glass. Who knows what I'll read? The announcement of my death, perhaps. The birth of a grandchild (not possible). Yet there's a hint of consolation coursing through it all. He knows I can't take much more.

His insights about art are fascinating, original. He's composed a manifesto, even. He calls it the "The Art of Disillusionment." He says he admires me because I'm one of the disillusioned. I've earned the honorific because of my ability to see him and his tribe. The Little : People don't appear to just anyone. Adam assures me only a handful of us are so blessed. Because, while The Little : People are everywhere, they don't readily let on. People are ignorant, and a little stupid. It's a pity. He and I go back and forth on these theories. I believe art should enchant. I believe it should take us out of ourselves and fill us with it-ness, and visions of alternate worlds.

Turns out Adam knew Susan Sontag. In fact, they were such great friends, he says she used to carry him around in her pocket wherever she went. Apparently, she took him with her to Sarajevo. He heard the cellist playing Bach while snipers ripped the city apart. He even claims to have fed her a few ideas, such as the one about the need for an erotics of art. It's not something I've ever properly understood because, Adam tells me, Susan did such a poor job of explaining it. He said he spent hours trying to clarify how a sentence could act as an aphrodisiac or a hallucinogen, and that taking it apart for hidden meanings missed the point. He quotes Emerson at me: "The art of life consists in skating across surfaces. He who goes below the surface does so at his own risk." When he said it, I almost fell off my chair. "You can't sit in the future," he added.

Adam's politics are hard to follow. For example, he loves David Brooks. Like, how is it possible that the author of *Bobo's in Paradise* speaks so forcefully to him? One of us is playing the other – but who? Adam is imagining a character named Adam who has an affair with his daughter, Katia.

But I know for a fact what's really going on between him and his sister, Grisha. The truth is, I too lust after her. Everyone does. Does the word slattern say anything to you?

*

I don't delude myself into thinking the Little : People actually need me. They've been around forever, after all. They're old as life itself.

The Little : People will embrace anyone into their ranks – even though almost no one sees them. They're non-denominational. Everyone who wishes to be one of the Little : People can enlist, so long as you're not a robber baron or carpetbagger, of course. Because, while they aren't ideological, the Little : People, if they have any enemies, well, it's plutocrats who, for some reason, hate them. The Little : People are progressive – LGBT rights had been achieved among them generations ago.

There is nothing not to like about them. They're the perfect people in a highly imperfect world.

They are born in the air as bacteria and alight in dark, obscure places – such as closets – where they incubate and hatch. They have always been here – as long as we have – and they're everywhere.

But no longer with me. I can't afford their friendship. The end times are upon us and I must act accordingly.

Gogol's Noose

"Oh, mama, imagine it – Gogol is sitting here in the cup." You rushed from your place and cried: "Where is Gogol?" Liza undertook to catch him with a spoon in the glass and shouted anew: "Oh, it isn't Gogol, it's a fly!"

Nikolai Gogol, in a letter to E.G. Chertkovna

The best of all things my pen has produced ... it will reveal, if only in part, the strict secret of life and the most sacred heavenly music of that secret.

Gogol

The unearthing of this early manuscript, which happens to be the only work he ever wrote in Ukrainian, is of inestimable scholarly value. This futuristic fantasy, whose title may loosely be translated as "My Noose", may well be the strangest thing this strangest of writers ever produced.

St Petersburg, 1834

Finally the door opened. A scab-faced servant bent to the waist and scampered out of sight. There, dimly visible by the hallway's candlelight, robed in black, stood the silver-bearded Bishop. Gogol crossed himself and bowed to kiss the outstretched hand. The Bishop's fingers were long and tapered. Gogol's sensitive nose detected an unusual smell: was it possible Father had been playing stink-finger? He eyed the blond servant girl staring at him over the Bishop's shoulder.

Unable to resist, Gogol dropped to one knee: "Bless me, father, for I have sinned," he began.

A heavy hand capped his forehead. "I hope so," muttered the Bishop, purple skufia angled rakishly atop his head. Then: "Not here, young man, not yet. Now, get up."

Startled by the prelate's levity, Gogol straightened. He'd been expecting banal aloofness, not plausible wit. He was distracted by what sounded like birds chirping in the next room. The palace, he knew, had been built in the time of Ivan the Terrible. The ceiling in the cold gray stone hall soared thirty feet or more, its timbers ambered with stars.

"This way," the Bishop said. He led Gogol toward the bright light pouring through an open double-doorway, into the adjoining room.

Unused to such brightness, Gogol blinked repeatedly. The light came from what must have been a thousand candles, in sconces, on tables, along the walls, in wagon-wheel candelabra, and standing torchieres mapping the room. All illuminated its singular feature.

Suspended from rafters on ropes of gold braid hung several dozen gilded birdcages, each confining a pair of nightingales. The gray- and buff-colored birds eyed the intruders anxiously. At that moment, the Bishop reached out and yanked a red silk cord, also suspended from the ceiling. From high above, a bell sounded.

Then, lightening: the nightingales in the cage nearest the door started to sing. Within seconds the song was picked up by the birds in the adjoining one, then the next, and so on. By the time they'd reached the center of the room, all three dozen birds were singing. Gradually, their random chirping synchronized. Gogol noted bits of melody. The tone and harmonies were a rich, earthy brown, washed in umbilical mist, reminding him of St Basil's own cathedral choir.

Yes, no mistaking it: the birds were singing a morning hymn in Old Slavonic.

Gogol crossed himself three times. To be in the presence of such a marvel was more than he had ever imagined. And they listened in silence as the birds moved through the ritual tune, hailing the sun, and welcoming the risen Christ into their lives.

Outside, the moon plashed its oar in the Neva. But it was the image of the Bishop that haunted: the prelate stood frozen, but for a hand stroking the thin cranium of a large Afghan hound who'd slipped in from who knows where. The Bishop's head tilted, eyes shut, lips twisted in a scornful smile, the very picture of self-regarding ecstasy, as though the birds were singing about him.

The Early Years

GOGOL'S MOTHER'S FIRST two pregnancies ended in miscarriages. When she learned she was pregnant again, she had a church built to secure the budding being's health. After Gogol was born, she took him to mass daily. Staring at the icons of Mary cradling her son, she clutched the infant Gogol ever tighter. She monitored his every sniffle, cry, and whimper. For his own safety, she did all she could to tame him. Taught him virtues, fear, and consequence. Her impromptu sermons about hell were painted in blood and fire. Meanwhile, his grandmother harrowed him with goblins, witches, wolves. He sparkled, listening, loving the uneasiness the stories stirred, the cheap thrill of fear. He tested their truths. Once, a cat jumped out of the bushes and scared him. Recovering, Gogol grabbed it by the tail and hurled it into the pond. When it attempted to crawl out, he pushed it back time and again until it finally drowned. Afterwards, he began hearing voices in the dark calling his name. Like many of his generation, he had an experience of the void, of the nothingness concealed behind appearances. It chilled and fueled him.

His first book, *Hans Kuechelgarten*, which he burned, just as he would his last, the legendary sequel to *Dead Souls*, was about a dreamer who scours Europe in quest of the beautiful. Transfixed by the ruins of the Acropolis, he concludes that humans are contemptible and that true beauty dwells within. It's a place he'd come to time and again.

After burning all the copies he could find, he decided he needed to visit America, "that fantastic country of happiness and rational productive labor". Using the money his mother had sent him to cover their estate tax, he bought a ticket to London. Soon after boarding the ship in Luebeck, he discovered no one on it spoke either Russian or Ukrainian. Here's where it gets interesting. All official biographies have advanced the canard that Gogol got so seasick he jumped ship at the first port of call, in Germany. That's not what happened at all.

*

Gogol's appointment to teach World History at St Petersburg University represented an opportunity not to be missed. Gogol, boy from nowhere, a *lecturer* at the *university*! About World History he knew little. To keep his students from discovering this, he cancelled classes. On those rare occasions when he found it necessary to show up, he drew on his imagination to construct his lessons. Imagination fills all gaps in knowledge like tar.

He stressed the impossibility of actually "knowing" history. The problem was closely related to the impossibility of understanding life itself. It is a paradox of being alive that you simultaneously feel you don't really know much of anything about yourself and your circumstances while also recognizing that you are perhaps the only thing you can know, and that you are the only one who can know you from the inside out. For all that, you still feel like an amateur when it comes to self-knowledge.

Behind his stabs at self-examination lay a question: how much of his destiny was actually in his hands? How much of his life was arranged for him by others? Who, if anyone, defined the context in which he, and others, lived?

*

"Fiction," Gogol speculated aloud, while his students dozed or wandered out of the lecture hall, "is a method for organizing facts in a way that renders them memorable." A girl wearing a stole made of wolf pelts cinched at the neck with a pearl clasp sighed loudly, pushed up from her seat, and stomped out.

"It evolved out of earlier oral traditions in which the mnemonic devices of poetry became a way of embodying time," Gogol continued, oblivious. "Oral histories were altered by every subsequent narrator: changed, embroidered, unzipped. The genealogy of Hesiod's gods became the springboard for Homer's more flamboyant cast."

He took a bow for that last pithy remark, then continued.

The three remaining students looked at each other: they understood what he was saying, even if their ignorant classmates remained clueless. The departed were mainly children of nobles and wealthy merchants who had no need of mnemonic devices for passing time. Those who stayed were scholarship kids, bruised by life's apparent contradictions, starving for whatever light the beacon at the lectern might shed on the devouring darkness around them.

Gogol barely noticed the posse of bones huddled in the back of the hall. Cocooned in dreams, he grew more expansive as the room emptied, filling the vacant seats up to the mullioned windows with golems and ghouls sprung from the cauldron of his brain. He could barely hear himself speak above the clamoring crowd.

"Plato," Gogol preached, "marked the tendency of memory and imagination to mingle, forcing philosophers to winnow fact from fiction, hunting the reality beneath. The apocryphal became significant by stirring the imagination."

Which was a step too far even for his diehards, who slipped, unnoticed, out of the hall and into the common light of day.

Dead Souls

1842. Disaster. Publication, or the death of the soul. It was better when he was unread, unknown, unmolested by impious eyes and their banal judgments. Before, he'd been free. Suddenly he was famous – that thing all writers believed they desired until it arrived, a bitter destiny. Fame birthed all manner of misunderstandings, like Venus spawned from the sea and doomed to seduce all who saw not through but with their eyes, who devoured the skin, the surface, the outline, without ever knowing the core, the heart and soul of the matter.

Gogol sat in his room, poking at his stove, a sheaf of pages stained with his meticulous script – he should have taught penmanship. Now *there* was a manly vocation. Instead, driven by ego and vanity, he chose to tell the story of an empire which, like all empires, survived by eating its young and thrashing its poor. He watched the coal glow orange-red and he imagined a phoenix, a bird of fire, suddenly bursting out of the black cast-iron bulb spitting and hissing before him.

Well, he had asked for it, had he not? Readers believed he was speaking to them, for them. Absurd. He could barely speak for himself.

Suddenly he had an urge to reach in and grab a lump of fiery coal and squeeze it in his fist.

His confessor was right. Art had more to do with the Devil than with God. He loathed admitting it, but truth had always been his muse and he wouldn't hide from her now.

He would have to escape to Rome, that ephemeral city, that modern Babel, to which all roads eventually led – if, that is, one were looking for power. Not so, Gogol. Earthly powers were what he sought to escape from above all. He wanted a glimpse of the holy; he wanted that more than anything, with an intensity that pulsed like a madness.

He rose and paced the dark room. Well, now he could afford more luxurious quarters – that, at least, was something, no?

No one understood his title. *Dead Souls*. It was he himself who had died. By exposing his innermost self to strangers, by inviting their gaze, he had crucified the key part of himself and he would never get it back.

He stared out the window at the snow. It was one of St Petersburg's celebrated white nights, when the light never quite went out, and the whole snow-covered landscape shimmered as if under the lights of a million candles. Oh, the environs had their charms – none quite as startling as the Amber Room in the Catherine Palace in Tsarskoye Selo, where Pushkin had taken him. Imagine: an entire room with walls of carved amber, the flawless work of German craftsmen, six tons of it, like nothing he'd ever seen. Power dictated to beauty, this was the tragedy. It enraged him. He'd had enough of the paradoxes of success, enough worldly temptations. Enough.

He marched briskly to the stove and stared into the amber-colored flames. Without hesitating, he thrust forward his hand and seized a burning lump the size and hue of a sizzling orange and squeezed it in his fist like a mouse he was strangling. Why that came to him, he had no idea; but that's how it was with extreme pain. Suffering was one of the greatest ways of making discoveries. He'd let this stone from the bowels of the earth sear the flesh of his pale, intellectual's hand for which he had such unalloyed contempt, and never once would he give the world the satisfaction of tears or cries of despair. Some things he saved only for God.

Gogol's Noose Tightens

In 1842, Gogol, having overseen the publication of *Dead Souls* in St Petersburg, returned to Rome. He'd gone there to escape a self which had become odious to him. Himself had become "a famous author". Gogol was thirty-three.

After chaperoning his novel past the censors without sacrificing too much of its bite, he was ready for something new. Notes toward a sequel filled the blue steamer trunk at the foot of the bed. Sunlight slatted crosses over it through windows taller than the house in which he'd been born. Gogol bent his neck back, gazed blankly at the hotel's lofty ceiling, painted white and ornamented with guilded plaster mouldings, and lit his pipe.

He could touch his nose with his tongue. His hair, thin and greasy, fell straight down over his temples. His former student, the future novelist Turgenev, said he looked like a clever, sick, strange creature. Annenkov, on the other hand, claimed Gogol's face had acquired the rare beauty of the thinking person: thin and battered by ideas, with long, thick hair, and blazing eyes. Like all geniuses, G was a chameleon.

There was still the matter of his virginity. He'd heard the rumors, persistent enough to have rounded back to him, that he was malformed, impotent, a homosexual, and a religious fanatic.

They were all true, of course. He was all those things. So what? He was also many other things. He was the universe entire, but so what? Nobody's business but God's. He hadn't traveled to the eternal city to explain himself to men.

Men – he emptied his pipe into a beaker of green Venetian glass – men were bitter beings. He could no longer abide them. Certainly he didn't want to return home. He couldn't countenance the slavery on which the Empire, like all empires, had been built. He believed that by staying in St Petersburg, by enjoying the fruits of his success, he participated in the world's evil. He was himself the son of a slave owner. He supported serfdom yet he hated it. He could not make sense of his own ideas. He wanted an end to cruelty, and made his contribution in the form of a novel.

He wished he had Pushkin's nerve. Pushkin warred with czars while Nikolai, intimidated by the consequences of dissent, wrote dithyrambs in their honor.

He glanced at the newspaper on the table. At last! Alphonse Ratisbone's conversion was deemed genuine, "instantaneous and perfect" in the words of Cardinal Patrizi. After all, it had been brought on by a miracle. The banker's son, who'd recently been given a medal depicting the Virgin by a Catholic friend, later accompanied that friend to the Church of St Andrew of the Thickets, and there it happened. Almost immediately on entering he saw the Virgin herself, in a pose resembling the one struck on the medal. The church flooded with light and he felt himself enveloped in an atmosphere of infinite mercy, and, in his words, the veil dropped from his eyes. All the Hebrew wisdom of his sleepy youth evaporated in a flash of light. Having beheld the truth, he had no choice but to follow it. It took the church more than a decade to ratify the miracle, but there it was, in black and white, the whole story, in the newspaper on G's table!

Because the only beings who interested him any more

were saints. Philosophers were mostly brutes and fools. Descartes dissected living dogs to prove that man alone was sentient and suffered pain. The poor beasts howled like automatons – or so they sounded to him.

Gogol sighed. Another sign that Rome was where he was meant to be. He flipped the newspaper over. Now if only he too might be granted a visitation equally definitive, he could go on with his life. He scratched a fingernail along the walnut tabletop, already scarred by centuries of pilgrims.

As a young man, he believed books changed the world. Now he wasn't so sure. Books were the consumer goods of the upper classes, the pastime of housewives and ladies of leisure, of weak-willed young men who convinced themselves they were accomplishing something useful merely by reading when all they were doing was stretching indolently across a bug-infested mattress, stuffing their overheated brains with increasingly perfervid fantasies while, outside, wind and rain lashed the poor without mercy.

The cycle was obvious: the young serf quits his hovel at dawn to start his fourteen-hour day, while the wife and hatchlings scramble toward their own chores amid rioting chickens observed by a goat atop the wheelbarrow. Yes, animals were *their* slaves. The serf returns after dark in a depraved state of mind, body spent, soul squelched, and what can he do but discharge his rage on the wife and kids? Gogol's own father, a grandson of Cossacks and priests, received hundreds of serfs in dowry. And this trafficking in bodies has gone on for centuries while the nobles and the literati pursued meaningless activities designed to raise their reputations and status. They believed they'd earned their privileges. By the sweat of their brows. Well, clearly it's the sweat of someone else's brow.

Gogol's mother never knew he used to sneak out of his room at night and wander down to the ring of straw-roofed shanties below. While the main house slept, the serfs cavorted. He crept among the houses, peering through windows, watching peasants dance the hopak. He'd tuck his long ear to the wall and listen as husbands made love to wives, and wives berated husbands. Sometimes he'd luck out and catch a young girl undressing; other times, it was a boy he watched stroking himself. Why, then, did everything human seem alien to him? Why did all these so-called normal pursuits, which the entire world accepted, strike him as primitive and shameful, if also infuriatingly absorbing?

This thought flowered and grew vivid in Gogol's mind, because at that moment a servant, a pretty, darkish Italian girl with a faint shadow under her nose and a smile both winning and evasive, entered the room to make his bed.

Gogol looked away. He shuffled papers so violently he knocked over the inkpot, blotting it with his sleeve so the girl wouldn't notice. Of course she did. He thought he heard her snicker.

He had a hard time settling down. Demons pursued him. He woke early and reached for his pen at once, to reconstruct his dreams.

May God preserve you from haemorrhoids, was how he greeted folks these days.

He'd never been able to be around people unless he felt perfectly free. The problem was, people cast their shadows over you like nets, even though they meant nothing by it. But if you were in the least bit sensitive, these shadows slowly strangled and finally destroyed you.

The servant came and went without a word. Only that immortal snicker. She knew him well already, and he'd been here less than a week. Again, he cursed himself. Why had he lost his nerve? He needed company, needed to unburden himself to someone. He missed his dearest Alexandra like a limb. She was due to arrive any day. Not soon enough. He would write her a letter, urging her to hurry.

He probed the still-warm pipe bowl with his pinky, sniffed it, set it down again, and walked over to the window.

He had a misshapen stomach, which accounted for a lot. It made everything different for him. He had to watch his diet like nobody's business. No one with a healthy constitution would ever grasp his POV. He would die alone.

He breathed on the pane and quickly scribed a Cyrillic A on the glass he watched evaporate, revealing the street scene below. His eyes locked on a family of five standing in a circle on the corner. Three small children surrounded the woman, who seemed to be having a heated debate with the very tall man. All five wore black hats that made them look like members of a singular tribe, a secret society, the Sect of the Black Hat. Gogol imagined the woman accusing the man of making eyes at her sister over dinner the night before. The man replied by saying it wasn't his fault if he desired the things a healthy man commonly desires of a woman. At which the woman sneered, turned, and marched away, kids trailing her like anxious goslings. Brava!

Men in perfect health were monsters. They had no idea what it was to be vulnerable before your own body. Those who didn't know him well mocked his delicacy. Oh and the issues around diet! Last week he'd gone to a doctor who prescribed leeches, and Gogol let the fool apply the bloodsuckers – but at the end of the treatment, which was hideous beyond belief, he began to weep. Memories of his mother and of his childhood flooded in, and he realized that this doctor was out to destroy him. As were most doctors. It was the nature of their profession to destroy their patients while pretending to cure them. In reality, they despised illness, which was why they became doctors, and they hated those weak enough to succumb to it even more – these willing hosts to horrors, unable to repel the germs that swarmed in the midday air. Satan's minions, each and every one. Physicians were themselves often little more than servants to disease. That doctor was out to destroy him. These simpletons of the body who failed to grasp the way the universe worked, who didn't believe in the Devil eternally striding with invisible majesty across the landscape.

He leant his forehead against the glass, the better to see the streetlife below. No sign of the feuding Black Hat clan. Only the usual parade of cravats and waistcoats, with an occasional early gown of watered silk to sweep the angel dust off the fountain rims and into the air. Bursts of light, every one.

The Devil was invisible to everyone but Gogol. Gogol saw him as clearly as he saw the Colosseum and the Forum, though, frankly, they all looked so fragile and tenuous that he imagined them suddenly loosening from their moorings, to soar into the air, hurtling through darkness toward the source of all light, only to be melted by the sun. He saw the Capitoline Museum flap its wings and fling itself skyward, joined soon by the Pantheon and all the other ruins of that wretched, pagan empire, leaving him surrrounded by a vast wasteland, a field of precisely nothing – the red earth that was here when Rome was Rome, and even before, the same stuff in which Romulus and Remus played after suckling on the she-wolf who nursed them, growing strong under the sweet Italian sun, the do-wop dolce tender light. That's the Rome he saw in *his* mind most mornings. Because these blights of power held no gravity for him. As for the rest, well, there were Peter and Jesus to think about, and that brings him to the matter of his confessor.

This confessor, he was something else. He never sweated, no matter how hot the weather, no matter how much liquid he drank. Wasn't that curious? The body was a mystery. He was a priest, a holy man, severe and urgent. He was gaunt and earnest and loved the smell of suffering. Gogol's friends wondered how Gogol survived this shaman's ruthless ministrations. However, another kind friend visited regularly, coming by late afternoons so Gogol could dictate the next installment of his new book.

Oh, a knock on the door! There he was.

If the Devil had a Lover

TO RESUME: When that part of my life was over, when the Devil and I had parted ways – the Devil was in me, I know it – I had to begin again. But first I had to find that point, that place inside from which I wouldn't stray, because I couldn't, because it was that fixed point in the whirling world before which others knelt, to which they prayed. I needed nothing less before I'd trust myself again, or ask another to. The still, pure point, *nolens volens*; I was going to take it, beat down the walls that separated me from it, at least once in this lifetime. I was alive, and I wanted to see God – was that too much to ask? No! It was what we are born for!

If what sages of all traditions agreed on was true – that the kingdom was within us – then I knew just where to look.

Besides, what's a Devil without a God?

*

Alas, Gogol couldn't stay focused for long.

Dearest Alexandra,

I have always wondered how it is that more historians don't commit suicide – that it's the poets who seem driven toward self-destruction. When you consider how impossible it is to map with any depth and honesty the contours of a single consciousness, you realize that all historians are fantasists and, more, liars of the greatest magnitude. They keep pretending to speak authoritatively about the movements of masses of people across huge expanses of time, yet it doesn't take more than a moment's sober reflection to realize that such claims are six shades darker than black. Absurd. Translating the murmur of immemorial bees sounds positively scientific beside it.

In your letter you ask why I don't simply join a church. Wouldn't that "solve" my problem – address my need for community? By which of course you mean spiritual community, which offers training in the path to sainthood, and prepares us for what may – or may not – await us in the afterlife. I can answer your good question, though the answer itself may not please you any more than it satisfies me. But one's nature is one's nature, and there are only so many elements within it that you can do something about. And this is one against which I'm powerless. Explain it to yourself as you wish. Blame it on the fact that I'm Ukrainian.

Whatever the reason, the fact remains that whenever I hear of a church, no matter how esoteric, espousing Gnosticism or orthodoxy or some obscure occultism, I laugh – as though truth were susceptible to codification.

And as to how "they" (the government, who else?) will use me – they call me a realist, can you believe it? A social reformer! What drivel. What fools I'm surrounded by. But I see the future, I see my country's future unfolding naturally out of its past: I see the peasants, former slaves, rising up and destroying their masters, slaying them, raping their women, eating their children. Four centuries of oppression will require an orgy of bloodletting as expiation, don't imagine it will take anything else. Once the monsters have spent themselves – having utterly surrendered to their appetites – they will find these appetites may be sated, and have an end, and yet life itself continues, as the Romans discovered. We're either eaten by our children, or we end by dissembling the old truths, which never become irrelevant.

O but Italy – a dream to be here. My first poem, how could I forget, was titled Italy – but I published it anonymously, I was eighteen, what did I understand of fame? Later there was "Hans Kuchelgarten". Things German were all the rage. 1829. My prospects weren't good. A reviewer essentially called it a smelly crap. I immediately went out and bought up all the copies. I didn't want the public to see me as a failure before I began. I took all the copies I could find, rented a room at an inn, and burned everything in the fireplace.

But all that is behind me now. The sequel on which I'm working, while also a fantasy, bears little resemblance to the first volume. Something keeps luring me away from familiar times and places, into a country and a future which can only be imagined as unfolding in that mythical new world of the United States of America in the 21st century. Two centuries and seven thousand miles away. Inevitably, I've given it some features of our present-day nightmare. For instance, as you know, we landowners pay no taxes, yet our peasants, who work our land for us, do. It is a clever system: those who work must pay for the privilege. That's something I believe will carry forward into the future.

I hope you won't mind if I send you a few pages of the new work now and again. All I ask is that you respond honestly. If something strikes you as off – I count on you, as I always have, to let me know.

Above all, hurry! There are no humans left in Rome. Only cani e Americani, as the locals say.

From the Notebooks

Fortunately, Romans have no freedom. Grown lazy under the popes who rule them, they submit to authority as docilely as dogs. What I love about Gregory XVI is his hatred of liberals, along with his contempt for every democratic impulse whose ultimate end, after all, is nothing short of regicide.

To defile a beautiful mind. That seems the world's chief goal.

My own reduced circumstances – my, I can say it, poverty – are largely the result of my own choices, as were most things, so I blame no one, though there are systemic flaws creating roadblocks where exits should be clear, signs legible. It's an inspiration to me, my poverty, forcing me to summon the resources of my complete imagination with determined rigor. Poverty is my nearest of kin, though of course my poverty is itself relative. My mother owned many serfs.

I needed first to own up to my self. I'd gotten in over my head in Petersburg. I arrived eager to play. The natives looked me up and down – the famous once-over – and took a gamble. A new boy from the provinces, pining for the grownup sports. My vulnerabilities were clear. These city people moved through realities I'd never encountered. Everyone in Pushkin's circle came from a noble family, accustomed to privileges and a leisure I would never know. They could barely see me, I was so transparent, a loose sack of molecules lacking the necessary density to make me a full participant in their rough lives – but not unusable, not a complete waste. And so they used me, and so I let myself be used.

The Petersburg elite built palaces the likes of which they've never dreamed in England. Many had private theater companies and orchestras made up of gifted serfs whom they sprayed gold. Some had their own circuses. But I didn't care about any of that.

Pushkin alone interested me. With Pushkin, it was love. I don't imply anything undignified. My admiration for him was pure and complete, and my gratitude to him for noticing me – after all, I was nobody, a Gogol, a khokhol, while he was Pushkin, of the celebrated Pushkins, four of whom were signatories to the decree which enthroned the Romanov dynasty – my gratitude was boundless. He could trace his ancestry back to the times of Alexander Nevsky in the 13th century. The stories I know about Russia's greatest poet would fill ten cantos. His love for the girls, his eagerness to duel, his black blood. He spoke his mind no matter the consequences. He lay in bed all day and all night when it suited him.

"I can't live without her, you acknowledge that, don't you, my simple friend!" he once confided to a dozen of us at a dinner party, looking directly at me. "Unfortunately, she's a cannibal and I no longer have a heart." I nodded to my borscht, where I perceived the strangest reflection: my face appeared surrounded by red-winged demons nibbling my oily hair and dangling off the tip of my beaked nose. I looked around. No one else had noticed. This was how the demons work. Only their victims see them, adding madness to the case against us when we speak.

I asked him once, "My esteemed Alexander Sergeyevitch," I coughed into my sleeve and noticed I'd forgotten to button it. For the longest time I paused, reflecting on the matter, which was not inconsequential, no matter what the others say. I had by then forgotten my question. Seeing Pushkin's puzzled gaze, I blurted: "How's your mother?"

"Dying," he deadpanned. Seeing the look of horror on my face, he began to laugh.

"I'm teasing, my simple friend. She will outlive us all! It's her black blood, you know."

I did know. Everyone knew about his African great grandfather, kidnapped by the Ottomans and gifted by the Sultan to the Czar. Gannibal. A brilliant man, the only black man in St Petersburg, who rose on the strength of his own gifts, becoming an engineer, a general, and a trusted advisor, first to Peter, and later to his daughter, the Empress Catherine.

Pushkin's tutor was brother to the notorious Marat, the intemperate Jacobin who, by all reports, had been as reasonable as a monsoon and who ended, like so many of his gang, in a literal bloodbath, stabbed in a tub by while scrubbing himself of indelible sins. The brother was another matter. Marat's brother dressed well, and was a favorite of the Empress. Alone with Pushkin, he reminisced about Robespierre, whom he'd tried to cure of his philandering ways by enticing him to the venereal disease ward of the local hospital. It didn't take.

And, of course, Pushkin's personal servant and valet, Konstantin Sazonov, was a robber and a murderer. This was well-documented.

The Warehouse of Ancestors

But the wonders of Russia were as nothing to the splendors and mysteries of Italy. Together with his friend Alexandra, Gogol visited the estate of Count Farina, who owned the mountain above Cortona. The Count, a gracious, big-boned man, was said to be descended from a family who'd crossed the Alps on elephants alongside Hannibal. It was he who showed G a sight that remained the great astonishment of his life.

The grounds around the mansion, though extensive, didn't boast the usual manicured gardens. Instead, an 8th-century chapel stood in the yard, adorned with a small painting of a Madonna, said to be one of the few unrecorded Crevellis –

the Count refused every entreaty by so-called art historians who longed to paw it, claiming they alone had the authority to authenticate the work as genuine. "What do I care for their certificates?" he observed, opening the chapel door to reveal the first of his treasures.

No art historian, Gogol nevertheless observed that the piece, about the size of a prayer book, was exquisite and luminous, featuring the artist's singularly vivid palette, along with his insistence on endowing all his subjects with hawklike features. Mary looked especially Semitic – which G, who had recently visited the Holy Land, supposed apt.

After a sumptuous dinner, followed by a hike halfway down the mountain to visit the monastery that arose around a cave in which St Francis lived for a year, they returned to the Count's mansion, flush with a sense of virtue by osmosis, which they fueled with a drop of wine to dilate their happiness. Night had fallen.

The Count, who had drunk a bit more than a drop, suddenly leapt up.

"All right," he said. "All right. I trust you. I trust you both."

Alexandra and G looked at each other. What did he trust them with? They'd already seen the Crevelli. What else was he concealing from the world? Both noticed how the skin below his left eye spasmed like an eel.

"Come," he said. "I will show you something few outside our family have seen. Come."

And so they rose and followed him up the marble stairs.

At the top of the third floor, they reached a heavy door reinforced with black iron braces. The Count dipped into the pocket of his mauve velour jacket and removed a large, gold-plated key he inserted into the lock and turned. The door opened easily and they entered a room the likes of which G had never seen before.

The space was so large – cavernous, with long pine rafters ribbing the ceiling – that, despite the gigantic chandelier, much of the room remained in shadow. And the shadows were alive, shifting and rustling like bushes riffled by wind.

Entering, they heard a collective gasp, followed by a low moan. As G's eyes adjusted to the crepuscular light, he was able to make out human figures, bizarrely dressed in long silvery robes, so it appeared, sitting or sprawled on throne-like chairs around the room.

Gogol glanced at Alexandra. She just shook her head: *hush*. She was unrufflable, this enigma in silk, in a way only the rich and the French know how to be, but Gogol, attuned as he was to every flutter of this spiritual seismograph, noticed the slight catch in her breath.

Then they saw the chains. These – what to call them, forms? – were chained to posts in the floor.

As their eyes gradually focused, their minds seemed unable to clarify what it was they were seeing. They turned to the Count for an explanation.

"This is the Warehouse of Ancestors," he whispered, as a loud wail rippled in a wave through the room like the weeping of wraiths.

"Ancestors?" As usual, Alexandra was the first to recover her wits.

"They're all here, stretching back to Hannibal in the 3rd-century BC," he gestured at the gently swaying figures. "Immortality isn't the mystery it's been made out to be."

Gogol could feel the Count's pale eyes on his face. He clearly hoped for a reaction to this revelation but G was too startled to know how to respond. Both the Count's words and what G's own eyes were seeing made no sense.

"It's been available forever. To those who could afford it." Said with a smile both rueful and smug.

The blood returned to Alexandra's cheeks, and her breath came fast.

"May we speak to them?"

The count frowned and plucked the slope of his nose. He coughed. Instead of answering her, he said:

"Christ's crime was to make public what certain people had known all along."

Silvery sheets, low moans, a crescendo of sadness filling the room. G stared at the percussive, bewildering sight, brain blazing. Finally, Alexandra said:

"This is very interesting, count. But why can't we speak with them? I would love to hear how they report their experience. What is it like to live forever?"

"Alas, madame, if only that were possible. I share your curiosity. You note the chains?" Tipping his head.

"Yes, of course," she replied.

"I would be endangering you."

"How is that?"

"You see, madame, the truth is that while we long ago learned how to preserve the body, the soul is another matter. It turns out, you see, that it's the human soul which is mortal. After a century and a half, the soul begins to degenerate rapidly, gradually returning to an animal-like state. They lose the power of speech. They think and act like hungry wolves. Sometimes you'll hear them bark. Often they howl. It is strange and unfortunate. Unleashed, they attack, biting, scratching, and so on ..."

Gogol was no longer listening. The pale green moth which had been fluttering around had settled on his cheek. What was the significance? This disturbed him greatly. All things in the universe had meaning. This moth was no exception. It was perhaps the most important sign he'd ever been given – but, of what?

The Count, noticing his guests' reactions weren't what he'd expected, looked crestfallen. He coughed again, throwing out his arms as though to say: *Regard this room!* Finally, sniffling, he whispered: "Well, that's that. If you'll excuse me, I must get to bed now. We face the foxes at dawn."

Both G and Alexandra appeared relieved. Clattering down the stairs, they thanked the Count for his graciousness. They promised to come again, though of course they knew they never would, which comforted the Count, a little.

*

Later, back in Alexandra's room, Gogol tried to engage her on the subject, but she seemed uninterested. She paced, she rubbed an imaginary spot on her wrist. She seemed upset, as though she, who was prepared for anything, had not been ready for this – to have discovered immortality within reach yet maybe not within her grasp. Yes, he could see how this could be troubling, but why wouldn't she speak with him about it?

His brain teemed with the theological implications of "the visitation". So, death was an illusion after all? Was that possible? Had *that* been Christ's real message, and not this lesson of sacrifice of which he, along with so many others, had made such a fetish? Something about all this troubled him, and he longed to hash it over with the glorious Smirnova. Instead, he was cast back on himself.

He stood looking out the window for the longest time.

Then, after a silence that had become physically painful for Smirnova, Gogol leant back in his chair and delivered the strangest diatribe Alexandra had ever heard from him. He attacked language and praised the silence of animals. Why rob animals of the dignity they maintain by refusing to speak? May we learn from them instead ... if we do, we may yet become wise ... Nonsense in that vein for twenty minutes.

For a long time Alexandra said nothing. She rubbed her hands along her russet crinoline gown. She frowned and squinted at her rattled, gattling friend. She smoothed her voluminous black hair. Had she forgotten her handkerchief somehwere? Ah, well. What words would do when language itself was the scandal?

The next day, Alexandra Smirnova announced she was heading to Capri.

Letters

My Dearest Alexandra,

Success is only interesting to failures. Not that I had such a big one – although, by my lights, coming from where I did, it was plenty. Maybe I wasn't aiming high enough. But provincial ambition can be a poison, and I was determined – after a few stinkers, sure – to keep my focus on what mattered: freeing the spirit trapped inside the sable darkness of the flesh.

Do you remember the evening we met? It was May, a ball at Pletneyev's, the same night I was introduced to my glorious Pushkin, who had already celebrated your dark eyes in verse. He forgot to mention the velvet black hair parted in the middle, then bobbed into adorable earmuffs. He also called you the court's sternest critic. Little "pepper tongue". At twenty-two, a French girl born on Ukrainian soil, plucked from finishing school to wait on our Empress, you were adored and pursued by poets and princes. You were, and were not, one of us. Born of an old French line, you're lucky your mother was part Georgian, or you couldn't have managed us the way you did. You terrified me.

It was the summer of the cholera epidemic. Half the city emptied out. Only the poor remained behind to die anonymously in overheated homes plagued by mosquitoes and rats. Most of the poor dared not hope for more. And that's the goodness of the poor, from whom the rich have much to learn.

You terrified me, and I dared not pursue you. You were the prey of princes, who had every right to claim you as they did. A name is a destiny. Because mine means a kind of bird (the English call it a grebe), God gave me this beak for a nose, and wings wound of words. Hardly the plumage to dazzle a bird of paradise such as you. Our lifelong friendship is, to me, a testament to the truth of a bond that exists on a plane beyond the mundane.

That's why I'm writing to you now, to explain my choice. My decision to withdraw from the world in a way that's more final and extreme than even the path of the hermit monk is neither whim nor madness.

I don't wish to repeat the Pelagian heresy: human nature is not inherently good; sin is not a choice we make freely. We are entirely dependent on the Grace of God at every turn. No matter how much we struggle to be good, powers greater than we overwhelm us. The Devil dances through our minds and hearts.

I'm so glad we met again in this spiritual phase of your life. At thirty-three you're not a girl any more. And I, a whole year older, am well beyond the middle of my path – because I don't believe I'll ever know old age. My people have a saying: old age is no joy.

And how I shiver at your voice when I hear you singing those swift Cossack songs my father loved. We miss our Little Russia, don't we? The storks in the chimneys, the sour cherry pirizhke, halushkas with cream ... The rich tastes and aboriginal sights of home have disappeared inside the book of our secret history.

Forgive me for not kissing you that time you interrupted me while I was reading aloud from Dead Souls. *Not that I'm not charmed by breasts, but it is a long book, worthy of our full attention, and no romance is more demanding than the discipline of art, unless it be the worship of our common savior, Jesus Christ.*

After Jerusalem, after standing in the Savior's crypt, what else is possible but salt and prayer on my lips, followed by more prayer? We both have sampled the sweet dishes of the princes' tables, and they left our stomachs growling for some real sustenance, a spiritual food that might give meaning to our lives beyond our appetites.

That tree – a poplar? – outside the window is the spawn of decades of introspection and commitment. The tree focuses all its energy on being and becoming simultaneously. What it is and what it grows into is itself alone: it is an oak, or it is poplar. The present grows into the future and dies away with every stroke of my pen; the tree never grieves nor regrets it's not a willow, a rose, or a grackle.

When at last Dead Souls *was published, I was ready to move from Inferno to Purgatorio and from there to my Paradiso. Of course, a man can't write more than he himself has experienced in his soul, which was why I immediately tracked down Bishop Innokenti and asked him for his blessing on my works. He gave me them with characteristic generosity, together with an icon! Inspired, I immediately rushed to the friend at whose house I was living (he made the worst tea in Russia) and declared my intention to visit the Holy Land.*

The friends of my youth believed my only care was literature, but since my stay in Rome, and as a result of my most intimate experiences, experiences so deep I fear I'll never find the language in which to articulate them, my only concern is for my immortal soul. Purification must precede my travels, of that I am certain.

Did I ever tell you? It was long ago. I was a young man, just starting out, and overwhelmed by all that was expected of me – eldest son, head of a family with only two sisters for support in running the estate, and my knowing that I held a secret in my heart it was my obligation to drag into the light. It was the one thing I had to accomplish. Therefore, one Sunday – this was in St Petersburg, so imagine the backdrop of that Babylon you know so well – one Sunday I shut the door to my room and for an entire week refused to open it. For a week I did not eat. I would not open it, though my host kept knocking, begging, pleading, weeping. I refused even to answer – for I'd decided to go inward. I would get to the bottom of whatever it was I was, am, might still be. I prayed and meditated and refused to leave even when my mind rebelled.

Alexandra, I saw demons. I saw the hosts of Hell. They frightened me, but I refused to turn away. I stayed. I stayed until I felt I'd reached the final door – the door was in my mind, understand – and when it refused to open, I knelt on the stoop and prayed and would not leave. For days I alternated between prayers and obnoxious knocks until at last ... oh, it's almost impossible for me to say this for fear you might not credit my words. Mere words can never say what I saw next. And because I trust you, Alexandra, you alone will know that my efforts were rewarded: at a certain moment toward week's end, as I was knocking and praying simultaneously, the door burst open and I stumbled in.

What I saw can never be described. My words are shadows of a reality so grand and profound that you would weep for the rest of your days if you could only know a fraction of what I experienced there. The world beyond our world is brighter than a billion suns. It dwells inside us. This is the key to our savior's declaration: The Kingdom of God is Within. Yes, ecstasy beyond ecstasy, a knowing that is absolute, a universe of stars we're merely fragments of. That's what is there; it's what we are. I emerged illuminated. At that point, I could no longer contain myself. I burst open the door and rushed downstairs. My landlady, who was embroidering in the drawing room, heard my footsteps and leapt up. On seeing me, she screamed: Mr Gogol, your hair is on fire!

On fire, Alexandra! No, it wasn't fire: it was that ring of light you know so well from those icons you love. My sad pathetic head was crowned with a halo ... but I'll stop here, else I'll get too excited, remembering how I ran through the streets weeping. The sight of every living thing, each blade of grass, every leaf, brought tears to my eyes because I saw at last the miracles around me: everything has roots which sink beyond our earth into an elsewhere that's a hymn of light. Amen. I'll say no more about it. But it was then that I resolved one day to visit the Holy Land.

Two Days Later

In school they called me the mysterious dwarf. I recalled this, sitting in the grand office of Konstantin Bazili, the Russian ambassador to Lebanon, having taken three different ships to reach Beirut. Kostya happens to be my old schoolmate from the Nyezhin school. And he insisted on accompanying me to Jerusalem.

The road from Beirut to Jerusalem was rough. We crossed the Syrian desert on mules. Around us stretched a bleak and arid land. We passed Bedouins on camels and stopped in dusty villages where I spent the night exterminating fleas. My haemorrhoids acted up the whole way. Every step was a trial. By the time we reached Jerusalem, my nerves were ruined.

The city is controlled by Turks – outrage of outrages! Two Janissaries guarded the entrance to the tomb of the Holy Sepulchre. Once inside, I nearly suffocated. If there's spring to the step of my story, it's thanks to the Orthodox priest who sang the liturgy for me (and for a price) inside our Savior's tomb. Russian passersby on the street, hearing the priest's sonorous voice intoning God's mercy, Bozhe milostiv budy meni hrishnomu ... *began crowding in. I was so swept up in hearing the voices around me and imagining the Savior's body laid out on the rock that, though I prayed and chewed my lip, wept and prostrated myself, I felt nothing. My prayers were air, my tears the sweat of being, my knees obedient to earth, my mouth a well of blood. Somewhere in Samaria I picked a wildflower, another in Galilee. I stood on Golgotha and stared out at the Dead Sea. But there was nothing for me here. The truth was the Word, and it is the Word I have served my entire life.*

I've attached my final story. It's a visionary tale, dearest, and it begs the reader's indulgence. But I know no other way. It's also partly true, though I've no doubt you'll find it incredible. The first time I saw the Little : People I was just a boy. I found them by accident, in the barn, behind a bucket that held the horses' oats. Make of it what you will.

My one request: don't interrupt yourself while reading. It will spoil the effect. Indulge me this last time. Then write me. It's true that by the time your letter arrives I will be dead – in which case you don't even need to mail it. I will be able to read it over your shoulder as you write.

With all my love,
your g

Dearest Alexandra,

What if Jesus was ugly? My question might strike you as blasphemous but I am not being glib. I was thinking about what it meant for the Bible to say we are made in the Lord's image. I used to think that this didn't apply to me – because, well, you know how I look ... and then it came to me that perhaps our Lord was saying that we did not all need to look like the boys in Raphael ... So I ask again: If Christ looked like me, and artists rendered him honestly, would people still love and worship him?

Improbable as it sounds, I learned much growing up in Vasileyivka. I've told you before about Troschynski, the great landowner and former secretary to Tsarina Catherine II, who owned no fewer than six thousand serfs. We were lucky to have him as our neighbor. He loved both my parents, and we often spent months living on his estate. This provincial lord owned nothing less than Marie Antoinette's writing desk – which occasioned more than one lecture about what happens when our princes stray too far from the needs of those below them. His circle of friends was vast. It included several Decembrists, and of course Ivan Apostol, father to no less than three of those young madmen. You remember – or perhaps you were spared this piece of history? – they were soldiers, seasoned by their years of battling with Napoleon, who were tired of the emperor's caprices and sickened by the sight of their own family chained to their landlords' troughs by serfdom. Their rebellion could have been foreseen by a blind man.

The officers, sympathizing with their peasant troops, refused to re-enter high society as though nothing had happened, as though tens of thousands of serfs hadn't surrendered their lives to keep the invader from the gates of the city. They wore their swords to dances and scorned the high life they'd once loved.

But the courtiers rejected all attempts to abridge their privileges or temper their lavish lifestyles. So the officers, with one base in St Petersburg and another in Ukraine, mounted a coup. It failed. The plotters, like so many others before them, lived in an echo chamber. Speaking primarily with each other, they imagined they represented everyone. They overestimated the support they had among their fellow officers. Most of the radicals were arrested. Some were shot. Others got a thousand lashes. The rest were exiled to Siberia. Among the exiles was our beloved mutual friend, Pushkin, whose passion for reform, especially in his youth, knew no bounds. Incidentally, I hear the young Tolstoy is planning to write a novel about them.

I know you haven't approved of my political leanings in the past – but my conservative ways are no mere whim, I assure you. I have a terror of the mysteries we contain. My own desires are boundless. I flagellate them into submission daily because I am dying. I have stopped eating entirely. Maybe this will be my last letter. If so, don't despair. Be assured the good Lord has a plan for us all.

Your loving,
g

Also available from grandIOTA

APROPOS JIMMY INKLING
Brian Marley
978-1-874400-73-8 318pp

WILD METRICS
Ken Edwards
978-1-874400-74-5 244pp

BRONTE WILDE
Fanny Howe
978-1-874400-75-2 158pp

THE GREY AREA
Ken Edwards
978-1-874400-76-9 328pp

PLAY, A NOVEL
Alan Singer
978-1-874400-77-6 268pp

THE SHENANIGANS
Brian Marley
978-1-874400-78-3 220pp

SEEKING AIR
Barbara Guest
978-1-874400-79-0 218pp

JOURNEYS ON A DIME: SELECTED STORIES
Toby Olson
978-1-874400-80-6 300pp

BONE
Philip Terry
978-1-874400-81-3 150pp

GREATER LONDON: A NOVEL
James Russell
978-1-874400-82-2 276pp

Production of this book has been made possible with the help of the following individuals and organisations who subscribed in advance:

Thomas Bahr
Judith Baumel
Chris Beckett
Karen von Bismarck
Andrew Brewerton
Ian Brinton
Jasper Brinton
Peter Brown
John Cayley
Charles Capro
Martha Cooley
Claire Crowther
Ian Davidson
Stuart Dischell
Lila Dlaboha
Sharon Dunn
Rachel DuPlessis
Ginger Eager
Martin Edmunds
Charles Fernyhough
Allen Fisher/Spanner
John Fulton
Todd Gitlin
Andrew Grainger
Robert Gray
Paul Green
Penny Grossi
Charles Hadfield
John Hall
William F Hayes
Randolph Healy
Halyna Hryn
Peter Hughes
Dan Hunter
Diane Jones
Gene Kwak
Steve Lake
Lawrence Lee
Julia Lieblich
Richard Makin
Michael Mann
Megan Marshall
Jeffrey Masse
Lourdes Massing
Mark Mendoza
Thomas O'Grady
Toby Olson
Mark Pawlak
Sean Pemberton
Nicholas Ribush
David Rose
Lawrence Rosenwald
Lou Rowan
Dave Russell
Peter Sarno
Bob Scanlan
Lloyd Schwartz
Steven Seidenberg
Alan Singer
Katherine Snodgrass
Valerie Soar
Lloyd Swanton
Eileen Tabios
Troppe Note Publishing
visual associations
AJ Wells
Yara Arts Group
Andrew Zurcher

www.grandiota.co.uk

CPSIA information can be obtained
at www.ICGtesting.com
Printed in the USA
JSHW030840080721
16709JS00001B/9

9 781874 400837